Adventures with Almighty

An Allegory

Rebekah Schwep

INSPIRED FICTION BOOKS

Published by Inspired Fiction Books
501 Carter Lane
Ashland, OR 97520
Inspiredfictionbooks.com

Publisher's Note: This is a work of fiction. Names, characters, places, and incidents are a product of the author's imagination. Locales and public names are sometimes used for atmospheric purposes. Any resemblance to actual people, living or dead, or to businesses, companies, events, institutions, or locales is completely coincidental.

Cover Design © 2014 Cheryl Colwell
Adventures with Almighty/Rebekah Schwep. - 1st edition
Poem: Who Can Describe God's Grace? ©2014 Rebekah Schwep

ISBN:978-0-9892371-8-5

Who can describe God's grace?

It's running with horses in the violet wind

It's in my darkest, sickest, most loathsome sin

It's feeling me and stroking me and touching my face

It's beyond the bounds of sanity, dimension and space

There's no running or escaping this capture of the heart

It's a gift that breathes life, then blows you apart

Into worlds of untapped freedom and places never seen

It's a reckless adventure, it's a dream inside a dream

It's in the bloody, broken, stupor of a drunken, violent rage

It's in thoughts poured out in sweat and tears on a weakened page

Like glass scraping to ecstasy the hunger in my soul

It's the spark inside the blackness, it's the hope inside the hole

It's relentlessly aggressive, it's an aching at the core

It's addictive and obsessive, once you've tasted you want more

So, I sit by the gate where angels and demons congregate

And try to study things unseen, all the mysteries of the redeemed

And my soul begins to strive for rest, for the road to life that's paved with death

One day I'll be by the crystal shore, tasting life through death's door

From that perspective I will see, it was not my grip but His grip on me

And this gift beyond description, birthed from a bloody price

Will take me from near madness to a place called paradise

DEDICATION

I dedicate this book to Adam Schwep,

my awesome brother and my friend.

CHAPTER 1

PULLED OUT OF DARKNESS

I remember the darkness, the sickness and the sadness, the putrid smell of rotting flesh, the festering filth pumping though my veins. I wanted to take a blade and slice out every shameful thing that screamed at me from the crevices of my heart. Underneath the distractions and the stimulation, the depravity and the despair, I wanted to cut through my soul and find the hole causing so much pain.

In the middle of my misery, Almighty appeared. He would stand outside my door from one night to the next, day following day, and knock until the flesh of His knuckles bloodied and the strength deserted His arm. Sometimes, He left weeping, but always returned.

Having plummeted to my lowest depth, I began mocking His love, blaspheming His name and hurling His heart against the wall. It was at this point, that He spilled out His blood for me—in my darkest hour, in my deepest sin, in my most cowardly act. Yet, He knocked and waited, calling me by name.

In answer to His relentless pursuit, I finally opened the door and my life changed forever. The memory still chills me. He came to me in the night and pulled me out of my darkness into His light. When Almighty came to me and laid His hand of mercy on my soul, I became new. But that wasn't the end of the story, only the beginning.

There were issues and fears that inhabited my heart, present struggles and past condemnations that constantly battled for my mind. Almighty would find me and say, "Come, let us reason together. Come to me for though your sins were as scarlet they will be white as snow."

There lurked another voice inside me, the voice of Adversary. Sometimes I wasn't sure if this was in fact an adversary, a voice in my own head, or even the voice of Almighty. Nevertheless, whenever my heart deceived me, Almighty came with reassurance, setting my heart free with His truth. I grew to love Him and to love His voice. In our sweet communion, confusion always left, and peace settled into my heart and mind.

However, Adversary continued to hound my mind like a snarling dog, hungry for blood, sniffing for the slightest sign of weakness. "You know Almighty is not pleased with your wasting the many chances He's given," he would say. "As a dog returns to his vomit, so a fool to his folly. You are a fool. You've made no attempt to change yourself. You know how messed up you are. What makes you think Almighty would possibly accept you the way you are?"

How could I disagree? Some of my old ways were creeping back in, though I desperately wanted to rid myself of them. "I know," I said, despairing of my failed efforts. "If only I was different. Sometimes I think it's hopeless for me."

Adversary sneered, "Well, at least you know you are a worthless wretch. An unfaithful sin dabbler, who at one point was foolish enough to deceive herself into thinking she was accepted by Almighty."

My heart sank. I felt the truth in what he spoke, but was it the whole truth?

It was astonishing how many times Almighty labored in a myriad of ways to convince my heart of His love and acceptance. It's like I didn't get it. Or, I had altogether forgotten the words He had spoken. Or somehow, they would get twisted in my soul. Why couldn't I wrap my mind around the life-transforming truth that had changed me?

Occasionally I'd get a glimpse that I was focusing on myself more than Almighty, thinking that my badness was greater than His goodness. Thinking that the power sin had over me and the negative way I saw myself were more potent than His power to redeem me. I started to feel detached, losing my ability to reason, as though I had nothing solid to hold onto. I began to wonder how valid my emotions were.

Thankfully, Almighty came to me in that desperate place. I half expected it and longed for it, but my timid soul caused me to shrink back as feelings of unworthiness overwhelmed me. His strong voice surged like mighty waters, flooding my soul. I had yearned for the tenderness that resonated in His fear-piercing words. "Come to me. Come to me." It was an echoing whisper. "Come reason with me." It was like a beautiful, angelic song combined with a terrifying intensity that gripped my soul.

"Yes?" I stammered.

"I have something important, something revolutionary to say to you. So, I want you to listen."

I felt stunned by His directness. He hadn't been this abrupt—well, ever. "I'm listening," I whispered, anxious and a little apprehensive to find out what was so crucial to cause such urgency.

"Eppy." He said my name, sending prickles through my soul. "I love you as you are, not as you should be."

The words, simple and direct, pierced me. "How can that be? I don't understand," I argued. But no answer came. He had one message for me that night—a message He wanted me to meditate on and attempt to grasp.

In the days that followed, frustration mounted when I tried to wrap my mind around this reality and realized I couldn't comprehend it. Why and how came into my mind, and I finally came to grips with the fact that my own understanding was not going to cut it.

In my pondering, I came to know there is a word about Almighty, and the word is mysterious. He is unlike any being ever known to man, incomprehensively unique. He is a Being who strides to the beat of His own rhythm. As different as an artist is from a painting, so is Almighty's ways from the thoughts and ways of man. I got this about Him, or at least I was trying to. He is not indebted to anyone, does not need to go to anyone for advice. Mystery and glory are the very essence of His being. Good and evil are equally submissive to Him. He is uninhibited, to say the least. He is also an anomaly: We either love Him or hate Him. Those in between don't know Him.

When I tried to sleep, I would close my eyes and meditate on the words spoken to me, I love you as you are, not as you should be. The words continued to echo as I would drift off.

Not too long after that encounter with Almighty, something good began to grow in me—a seed of Almighty's love that He planted began to take root. I could sense, however, that the soil of my heart was not fertile enough to keep the seed alive. Along with the little seed of hope, dark visions thickened in my conscience mind. Unanswered questions and an awareness of self continuously presented themselves, attempting to choke the life from me. I harbored secret thoughts and frustrations, stuffing them down deeply so I didn't have to acknowledge their existence. I knew Almighty saw my corrupt heart, yet could still hear His gentle voice calling. "Come, come to me. Let us reason together."

One night, I awoke with a night terror. Breathing heavily, sweat streaking down my face, I dreamed I was hanging over the edge of a cliff, hot lava flowing below. My hands were slipping off the slick ledge.

"Are you okay?" Almighty's gentle voice called in the dark.

"I don't know. I don't know!" I said, wiping my sweaty hands on my sheet, perplexed at His calm.

"What don't you know?" He asked in a stronger voice.

"I don't know anything," I said like a child pouting. "I don't know what's going on inside me, and I don't know what you require of me."

"Eppy, let me explain," He said gently. "You are saved by works. They are just not your works. It is my works that have saved you. I did all the work for you on the cross. I don't expect anything from you. I don't even expect you to understand what I am saying to you. All I require is for you to trust in me. Have faith in me, the Giver, and become an ever-thankful receiver of my goodness. Remember when the children of Israel were in the wilderness and were bit by the serpents?"

"Yes," I replied, recalling the story.

"Then, you know Moses made a brass serpent and put it on a pole. If any Israelite was bitten by a snake, all he had to do was look at the brass serpent and he was healed. Many of the people didn't believe it would work. Some even did it angrily, but regardless, everyone who looked was healed. I became that serpent. I became sin for everyone, so all who look to me will be healed of their sin forever." He paused. "That's only half of it."

I wondered what He meant by that's only half of it, but I kept silent as He continued to speak.

"What do you think would happen if you let go of me?"

"I'd fall straight into hell," I said.

"Is that what you think?"

"It's what I know, absolutely."

"If you let go of me, I'd still be holding onto you. It is my grip on you that is your salvation. And I will never let go. I made a covenant with you, using my own blood, and I will never break it."

Unimaginable relief shot through my entire being, starting with my mind and ending with my spirit. There was a long pause between us, and I realized Almighty was still referring to the first half of the story. Curiosity sparked a fire of anticipation in my soul. "What is the other half?" I asked, wondering what more there could possibly be.

Although I didn't see Him, I felt His intensity as He studied me. I knew His next words were of grave importance. "I can't wait to tell you the other half," He said with great enthusiasm. "However, you must know not everyone will understand the magnitude of the riches of my wisdom and knowledge, nor the heights and depths of my love.

And no one can entirely understand it. My ways are past finding out. But listen as I speak and treasure the favor that is being bestowed upon you."

So, I listened.

"I not only took away the darkness that dwelt in you, but I've also replaced it with my goodness. I took your garbage and replaced it with my beauty. I wore your putrid rags of sin and in return, I clothed you in my righteousness. When I was on the earth, I lived a perfect life. I fulfilled the law perfectly, never sinning. I see you as if you lived my perfect life as well, always pleasing me—every hour of every day. I put my perfection on you."

"How can this be?" I asked. "You are not blind. Don't you see me for what I am?"

"I see what I choose to see. Because of my sacrifice, I am able to see righteousness in you where there was none. It's the Great Exchange: I take your bad and you get my good."

I thought back to my past. I had engaged in every imaginable vile and evil thing, none of which even began to describe the depths of the depravity of my mind. I couldn't think of a sin I hadn't committed. How could a past like that be replaced with perfection?

I wondered about all the people who had never committed blatant, obvious sins, people who lived good lives. Were those people able to offer up something of value to Almighty? Surely Almighty saw them as purer than me.

"Eppy," Almighty called, interrupting my thoughts. "Any of their own righteousness they would seek to offer would be as filthy rags, repulsive to me. They need my sacrifice as much as you do. Without it, they would be lost. No one is righteous, nobody.

"The cross is an offense to those who think they are good. It is the greatest symbol of the spiritual impotence of mankind. I'm not looking for good little boys and girls. The attempts man has made to offer anything of value from himself, is pagan, blasphemous and ridiculous.

What kind of offering do you think a person could scrounge up for me?"

I pondered those words and wondered what He wanted from me then. This was starting to sound both too easy and too hard. It was as though Almighty was on a whole other plane of thought. These concepts seemed as though they fell out of another dimension. My heart began to beat faster at the intense stirring in my soul. A spark ignited, and it started to burn.

CHAPTER 2

OBSESSED LOVER

"Eppy, Eppy," a hollow voice pierced the silence. At that moment, I didn't like the sound of my own name. Adversary hovered over me, and a dark cloud of oppression and fear accompanied him.

"You're so alone," he barked. "No one truly cares about you. If you died right now, you'd be briefly mourned and soon forgotten. The only one who might care is your ex-lover who wanted you sexually as well as emotionally. In fact, it might be worthwhile to look for him."

"I can't do that," I snapped. "Almighty delivered me from sin and darkness."

"Well, I hope you enjoy isolation, because no one cares for your soul, and no one ever will."

"What about Almighty?" I countered. "He has to care for me. He spilled His blood for me."

"He died for the whole world, Eppy, not just for you. How special could you possibly be to Him? Do you think Almighty really wants to take the time to be involved with someone like you?"

"I know," I moaned and clung to my bed, caving into His words. I sobbed for a few moments then became expressionless. Lying for hours, stoic and pale, I felt the life had been sucked out of me. Finally, I mustered up enough strength to call out to Almighty. The first time I called out His name, Adversary sneered, still hovering over me like a black cloud.

"Almighty," I called again in complete helplessness. This time adversary fled, but left fear and oppression behind to afflict me.

"Eppy," a voice called in the wind through my open window. "I am here."

I felt apprehensive. What if Adversary had been right? What if I was bothering Almighty with petty questions and stupid notions? Would He be angry? Would I become weary to Him? "I wanted to ask you something," I began slowly.

"Yes?"

"How do you feel about me?" I asked, immediately regretting the question. It seemed silly and trite, a waste of His valuable time.

"Are you sure you want to know?" He said.

"Ahh... I think so," I said, now not so sure.

He paused for a long moment, too long. "Are you sure you can handle it?" He asked again.

I hesitated, now less sure than ever. "I don't know."

"I want to tell you what's in my heart toward you, but I want you to open your heart to receive it."

"I will." Apprehension gripped me, but I listened as He spoke.

"I watch you like an obsessed lover. I watch the way your fingers and toes curl up when you wake in the morning. I see the way you roll out of bed and head out to work. I anticipate your expressions, your gestures, your smile. I am aware of all your frustrations, your passions, your fears, and your dreams. Everything about you, those things you like and dislike, I have created. I thought you into existence.

"I knew the effect you would have on people, both good and bad. The bad I have forgiven, the good I have inspired. My soul longs and agonizes for you with a passion that you cannot yet understand. My reason for dying was you and my reason for living is you. I am intent upon knowing you deeply and intimately and drawing you to myself. I dream about taking you out to the wilderness and speaking tenderly to you, giving your spirit a reason to hope. I will teach you about all the worthless things for which men hope. I will show you that the hope I will give has far more substance and is more tangible than anything in the visible realm. And that hope is me living inside of you."

There was a long, uncomfortable silence after Almighty had spoken. I had never heard Him speak with such poetry and passion. I couldn't believe the words were about me, with all my sin and sickness. I knew He could read my thoughts and the intents of my heart. They were often less than pure. Not to mention the blatant blasphemies of my past.

I knew my sins were forgiven. My past sins, my present struggles, and any future failures were covered by His blood. Almighty had drilled this into my head endlessly, with more and more intensity each time. But why would He bestow such passionate love upon me and be so detailed in His awareness of me? I realized if the reality of how Almighty felt about me truly sank into my heart, it would transform me beyond comprehension, and nothing else in this life would matter. And yet, everything would matter more than it ever had! I also knew I wasn't there yet.

In that moment, I realized something extraordinary about Almighty. Everything about Him was extreme and paradoxical: His fierceness, His tenderness, His severity, His kindness, His perfection, His becoming sin, His beauty, His marred appearance. He was everything altogether: fire and water, a destroyer, a savior, a warrior, a servant, a lion, a lamb. Almighty was beyond my finding out. This Being and the Creator of all creatures was like no other, and He had actually set His love upon me. His words, I watch you like an obsessed lover, caused tears to fall uncontrollably as I wept for joy, my soul filled with overwhelming amazement.

Even so, I was soon besieged with even more frequent visits from Adversary. He would come as a thief and steal the joy from my heart with his lies and deception. I was still so easily convinced, but each time, Almighty would appear and give me power and strength to restore me. I needed to stay under His protection, but sometimes I felt so distant. I blamed it on Him, but I knew it was me. I could feel myself running—I saw visions of it. In the evening, I would hear Him knocking on the door of my heart. Sometimes, when I refused to answer, it lasted all night long.

One particular night, Adversary lurked beside me with such a heavy despair that everything went silent except the beating of my heart and the ticking of the clock. Feelings of worthlessness washed over me. I tried to grasp onto truths and inject them into my soul like medicine. Unfortunately, as soon as I got my thoughts wrapped around one, it vanished. All I could see and hear were demonic wings flapping around me and casting shadows.

The words, Resist the devil and he will flee from you, came to mind. I called out to Almighty, but the demonic attack intensified. Then I began to speak words over myself that Almighty had spoken over me—words of grace and truth and hope. The demons left, although not right away. I closed my eyes tight, held my breath, and laid perfectly still.

When I opened them, Almighty was standing before me with arms open wide. When I saw Him, I felt angry. Why wasn't He there to rescue me earlier? He didn't know how severe it was. "I wish you could feel the ache that's inside me," I whimpered, brutally honest. "It hurts to smile. I feel a longing to disappear, to cease to exist. This pain is too much—I wish I was never born!" I glanced up and saw His smiling face. This made me more upset. Was I a big joke to Him, was my life a joke? I knew He cared deeply, but that knowledge didn't seem to help me in this agony.

"Do you realize who you are talking to?" He said, still smiling.

I didn't answer.

"I am a Man acquainted with grief, stricken with sorrow. People hid from me, Eppy."

It was the first time I had ever heard Almighty refer to Himself this way. He kept speaking, but I couldn't stop thinking of Almighty as a man.

"The ones I set my love upon turned on me," He continued. "The ones I opened my arms to beat me brutally. They repaid my kindness by literally tearing me to shreds. And the physical torture didn't compare to the spiritual torment I experienced in my soul. It was a level of anguish and isolation you can't comprehend. But you know what kept me going?"

"What?" I whispered.

"Thinking of you," He said. "You were the joy set before me. Thinking of my love for you and being able to redeem your soul pushed me on until it was finished."

At this point, I wanted to crawl into a hole and die, but for other reasons. I was so embarrassed at my stupidity. He kept staring down at me with eyes of love, still smiling. I wanted to speak, but no words would come.

"Your present suffering is not worthy to be compared to the glory I am bringing you into. One day your vessel of dishonor will be transformed into a vessel of honor, and we will be together forever, dwelling in unity and perfection. I am anticipating that day with great excitement. I can hardly wait," He said, the smile never leaving His face. And then He left, as serene, heroic and mysterious as when He had come.

I finally took a breath. I was awed. Almighty's words had such an impacting and transforming effect on my soul, I wanted to hang onto every word. I lowered my head, remembering how He had stood night after night outside my door, knocking until the break of dawn. And how, more often than not, I never opened the door.

CHAPTER 3

RUNNING AWAY

One day, it happened. I snapped. I couldn't handle the realities that battled in my soul. It was too much. The lies that had pounded on me year after year fought against the truths. I couldn't handle being so loved. I couldn't stand my own depravity staring me in the face.

So, I did the only logical thing I could think to do, I ran away—away from Almighty's arms, away from myself, and away from the truths that had set me free. I opened the door Almighty had relentlessly knocked on and darted out into the unknown, but all too familiar dark abyss of self. Whether I did this consciously or subconsciously I couldn't tell.

I had gone through too much pain. The trials seemed insurmountable, and I didn't want to fight anymore. I was done. And to be perfectly honest, Almighty was too eccentric for me. He was all too comforting and all too fierce. He was all together separate from everything I knew and understood. He had tapped into a vulnerable place inside me that I didn't want tapped.

I sprinted through the dark silhouettes of trees deep into the forest. The darkness swallowed me. The black night covered every shameful thought I had dragged up. So, I ran harder. I ran aimlessly for a while until a tiny flickering light appeared in the distance. I immediately ran toward the light. It was a compulsion, I was drawn to it. As I approached, the light grew increasingly bigger until finally I saw the silhouette of a man. He was the most beautiful, alluring creature I had ever seen. Another step and I recognized him. Adversary stood and beckoned me to come. I couldn't believe what I was seeing. He was different than I had ever known him to be. Seductive and sensual, he appeared as a stunning angel of light. He held out his hand for me to come. Instantly, a battle raged in my soul. I felt compelled to follow him, but a force inside me fought against the impulse.

Finally, I gave into the urge. I took hold of his hand, and he led me through the forest as his body lit the way. Ahead, a small cabin burrowed in the mist. He led me through the tiny door into the one room wood box furnished with only a table, two chairs, and a small lamp in the center. It looked like a place P.O.W's were taken to be interrogated and tortured. But for some reason, being inside this wooden cabin with Adversary felt comforting. I didn't have to take any risks or believe in anything or challenge myself in any way. I was protected from facing myself in this mirror-less room. And that was exactly what I wanted. We sat down at the table. I looked up at Adversary sitting across from me. I can't describe the beauty. It was surreal.

He picked up my hand, gently rubbed it, and began to speak. "I'm really not all that bad. I've only told you the truth about yourself, but you know what?" He gazed at me and continued, "You are a good person, and you should never feel like you're not. And I think you should know that Almighty's a total lunatic. He's an offbeat maniac with His 'When you're weak you're strong' nonsense. You need to stick with the familiar, and there's nothing wrong with that. Everything you need to make it through this life and be successful is found inside of you. You just need to believe in yourself. Trust me, you're stronger than you think."

I had never heard him speak this way to me. I have to admit it was making me feel kind of good. What if this was the right perspective? It sounded right, it sounded logical, and it sounded like common sense. It made me feel powerful and dominating.

Almighty once told me,' There is a way that seems right to a man, but in the end, it leads to death,' but what kind of statement was that? It sounded like a paradoxical parable which, upon reflection, seemed to be the genre that Almighty speaks in most of the time.

"You need to hold onto yourself and your inner beauty. Carve out a name for yourself in this life. After all, this life is all you have."

I have to admit the guy was starting to make sense.

"You need to hold onto yourself, Eppy," he repeated, "that's important."

When Adversary said my name, I felt lifted up at the sound. Maybe that's why Almighty loves me so much, because I'm special, because I yielded to Him, and because I'm good. I remembered Almighty's words,' The cross is an offense, it is the greatest symbol to our spiritual impotence,' but I quickly cast the words out of my mind. I liked the way I was feeling. Besides, Almighty should want me to be comfortable and experience pleasure on this earth. He must want me to be happy.

Adversary stroked my hand, sending shivers up my arm. He smiled, as though knowing my thoughts. "Don't worry about all those little things Almighty says are sin. He wants to put you in bondage. It's normal to do the things you were doing, at least some of them. You need to accept yourself the way you are. I accept you," he said seductively, leaning his face close to mine. He gazed at me, enticing me with his eyes.

Almighty was wild, a free spirit. He came and left according to His own free will. However, Adversary lingered with me in the safe cabin, comforting me with His words. He also kept me from risk and self-denial inside the secure boundaries he had set, but then he left.

I stayed there for days. I found myself swinging back and forth between justifying my own goodness while arrogantly judging others, to self-abasement, up and down like a rollercoaster. I felt sick from the inside out. And I sensed I was deceiving myself. I became fearful, closed off, narrow-minded, critical, and shallow. I avoided glancing at my face in the mirror. The tension mounted and finally, the deception broke. I knew I had trapped myself inside this cabin. I clawed at the walls I had created by letting sin seduce me, and now I was caged like a rat. I felt helpless, imprisoned by my own stupidity.

My only chance of escape was to cry out to Almighty. I hadn't spoken to Him in a while. I felt a nervous chill sweep over me. After working up enough courage, I said the word, Almighty, in a whisper.

"Almighty," I called out louder. Then out of desperation, I screamed His name. I heard the gallop of a horse in the distance. The sound grew louder as it approached the cabin. My heart beat faster and faster. I knew it was Him. As He approached, I felt excitement and terror. I didn't know what to expect.

He dismounted the white stallion and kicked the door of the cabin open, setting me free from my prison. Fury filled His face. His eyes were flames of fire. I was afraid to look into them.

I froze, unable to step toward Him, yet I didn't want to stay in this prison of bondage. "Almighty," I whispered.

He flung me over His shoulder and carried me out of the cabin, putting me on His horse. He was commanding and aggressive. I had never seen this side of Him, but felt safe under His authority, and terrified. Riding at an unbelievable speed, everything became a blur, and I couldn't see where He was going. Fear and adrenalin coursed through my veins, yet I realized I would rather be on this wild ride with Almighty, going who knows where, than behind the safe confines of the cabin of self.

He brought me to an enclosed meadow, surrounded by trees and wildflowers. One tree grew in the center. He pulled me off the horse, carried me to the tree and sat me down under its branches. Then He began to scold me. "What were you thinking?" He said, pacing back and forth, scratching His head in frustration. Yet under the surface, I recognized His grief.

"I don't know," I answered. "You always seem so tender and forgiving and..."

"Do you have any idea about the horrible repercussions that are brought about by sin?" His voice was unrelentingly tough. "There are gut-wrenching, heartbreaking consequences. You are mine, and I don't want to see you destroy yourself. I have a plan for you," He nearly shouted. "It involves risk and faith and adventure."

I burst into tears.

He gazed down at me, love flowing from His eyes. Then He knelt down and wiped my tears away with His hand. "My spirit yearns jealously over you," He said, softening His voice.

I looked at Him smiling at me, and in that moment, I wanted nothing more than to be like Him. He was filled with passion beyond reason. He had invaded me and there was no going back. I wanted to stay close to Him and commune with Him. I wanted His fire to consume me.

"Almighty," I said softly, feeling timid from His aggressive behavior.

"Yes, Eppy," He responded, sweetness calming His voice.

"How can I be like you?" I asked with childlike sincerity. "You're so different, there's nothing I could compare you to; you're so free. You're filled with passion and peace and rivers of love."

He stared at me, His smile becoming wider and brighter than I'd ever seen. Then He reached out and put His hand on my face. He pulled my head toward His chest and placed my ear against His heart. "Do you hear my heart beating?"

"Yes."

"It's beating for you." As He spoke, I felt my heart beat faster. "If you hear my heart, and you know my heart, then you know me. The more you know me, the more you will be like me. Keep your head always resting on my chest, and your heart will be in sync with mine."

I watched the sunset from under the tree while resting my head on Almighty. His scent was intoxicating—so potent, it soaked into me. Peace flooded through my entire being. "I wish I knew the secret to keep from wandering away from you," I said.

"I wish I knew that secret too!" He laughed, then explained, "Whenever you hear my words, I am there speaking to you, and whenever you call out to me, I am there listening to you. Whenever you distance yourself from me, I am there waiting for you, and when you run into sin, I am there grieving for you. Do you still not know my heart toward you?"

I rested in Almighty's arms and felt a twinge of pain as I thought about the question, knowing the answer. I didn't truly understand the way He felt toward me. I knew in my head, but it still hadn't penetrated to my heart—at least not enough to change my actions, or enough to keep me from being so self-absorbed. I couldn't even trust myself to stay and not run away again.

CHAPTER 4

REVELATION OF REST

The next day, I felt amazingly free. I felt a little of Almighty's freedom had been imparted to me. Just one night of being that intimate with Him had made a huge difference in my heart. I was starting to realize that hanging out with Him, being in His presence, was the key to my transformation.

I noticed something else. He was interesting. He liked to be sought out. He had told me if I drew near to Him, He would draw near to me. Also, He would let Himself be found by me, if I looked for Him with all my heart. It seemed strange, as if He wanted to play hide and seek. And then I observed lovers and I understood. I watched the way they played games with each other and teased each other. They tested each other in order to seek out a response. They played each other's little heart strings until they broke.

But Almighty was a phenomenon. He pursued with more intensity than I could ever think to pursue Him, and yet He waited for me to respond. Like an invisible intertwining, He was continually weaving my heart into His, taking my physical, carnal thoughts and morphing them into spiritual. Taking my temporal, shallow desires and making them eternal. I realized this was something only He could do.

I began meditating on this truth—He is the One who does all the work. The more I relaxed, the better off I was. In fact, it seemed the less I tried, the happier I was. But then again, it was Almighty who brought about victory, not me. So, if Almighty did all the work and brought about success in my life single-handedly, then what do I do? It seemed the less I strived, the more got accomplished.

I pondered this for several days, not because I wanted to, but because I couldn't get it out of my head. And then it hit me so fast and hard I nearly fell over. The answer was simple. It was encapsulated in one word, and that word is rest. That is the one thing I am supposed to do! Almighty was always going on endlessly about how He's done all the work for me, and how He just wants me to enjoy Him.

Yet, something about it didn't seem right. That couldn't be the answer. That couldn't be all there was. It seemed too simple and easy. I started to second-guess myself. I wanted to talk to Almighty about it, but the whole concept seemed associated with laziness or apathy. Yet, in another way, it seemed just like something He would come up with. I never knew what to expect with Him, and yet He was consistent and unchanging in His uniqueness, in His enduring love, and His eternal perfection.

I developed a growing obsession with the word rest and knew I wouldn't have any until I talked to Almighty about it. I also knew Almighty intentionally brought questions and concepts to my mind. Everything He did drew me to Himself. He had such a potent pull on my soul. I had to know what He thought about this. Whatever He said, I would commit my heart to—even if He said I must strive in labor with every fiber of my being and could only rest when I was dead.

I sought Him out, longing to reason with Him. At last, I found Him in a meadow sitting under a tree, the same tree where He had given me the whole spiel about sin and the painful repercussions. When He saw me, His entire face came alive with an expectant smile. He'd known I was coming. I had merely answered His call. There had been a few times I was convinced I controlled this relationship. You know, I was the one who had the upper hand. But then a moment like this would happen and wipe out that possibility entirely. I approached Him slowly, timidly.

His piercing eyes exposed every vain thought. I wanted to run away and hide from Him, but I also wanted to run to Him and hide in Him. "I've been waiting for you," He said when I finally reached Him.

"I know," I replied, kneeling beside Him. I think He was the only one in existence who was extremely approachable and extremely unapproachable at the same time. "I needed to ask you a question," I said softly.

"Well, I have an answer." He studied me, His face filled with anticipation.

"I've had this word floating around in my head and feel like it might be linked to something profound, but it is not a profound word, and I could be wrong."

Smiling, He looked down at His hands still bearing the scars of a debt long since passed. "What's the word, Eppy?"

"Um, the word is rest," I said sheepishly.

He gazed at me with eyes opened wide in surprise. "Say it again, louder this time."

"Um rest?" I said it more like a question.

"I've been waiting so long for you to come to this revelation."

I wondered if He had heard the word correctly. "Really, that one word is a revelation?"

"Eppy," He said in a serious voice, "I would shake heaven and earth for you to understand this one truth."

I stayed silent. Sometimes He spoke intensely, inviting an answer, but at times like this, I felt I should keep my words to a minimum. So, I listened.

"I am the Lord of rest," He explained. "Under the law, I made resting a command. Under grace it is a lifestyle. All meaningful accomplishment comes out of rest. Anything good that is done through you comes from simply knowing me, and the more you know me, the more you'll be at rest. The more you're at rest, the more will be accomplished. I give rest to the weary, to the burdened, to the striver, if they want it."

I wondered why He said if they want it. Why wouldn't someone want to be at rest?

"It's not the most natural thing for someone to embrace," He said, answering my thoughts. "People are more comfortable with earning and paying their dues. The problem is, they could never pay the debt they owe, even if they shed their own tainted blood and relinquished their own miserable lives. I had to find a creative way to deal with the situation," He said, glancing at the scars on His hands.

A shiver ran down my spine. I didn't know if I wanted to hear anymore. Everything He said held so much weight, it felt almost unbearable.

"The thing is, Eppy, resting in me is taking an alternate perspective on life. It's freedom. It's hard because it's unnatural. Rest implies trust. If you're at rest, you're not worried and you're not hurried. You've released all control, all self-effort, and self-glory. You become like a child, fully reliant and fully trusting. It does not mean things won't be intensively painful. In fact, sometimes things can be overwhelming, but it's actually possible to remain hopeful in the middle of horrible, nightmarish circumstances. Trusting me is the greatest compliment you could give me."

Sometimes I wondered why someone wouldn't trust a perfect, all-knowing Being who has proven His love to the point of the destruction of His life and extreme brutality to His soul.

"Why don't people trust you then?"

"There are many reasons—fear, doubt, discomfort with the unknown—but mostly it comes down to this, they don't really know me. They don't understand the depths of my love, the power I have to work on their behalf and my intention to do so. My devotion to each person is unparalleled by anything known to man. It is sad when they choose not to trust. Trusting in me has transforming power. It produces rest, peace, and hope—and hope does not disappoint because my love is poured out into them. It can completely change a person's perspective, their thought processes, their actions, and their life." He paused for a moment and looked off into the distance. "Eppy, do you trust me?"

I didn't answer. I didn't know if I could say yes in absolute confidence.

"You asked me once how I felt about you, I was just wondering how you felt about me?

"Well," I began, "You're unpredictable."

"Do you like that about me?"

"It definitely draws me out of my comfort zone. There's no one like You—You're indescribable."

"You know I'm crazy about you," He said.

"Yes, I'm starting to get that impression," I grinned.

"I long for your trust. I love it when you have simple childlike faith in me—it blesses my heart tremendously."

I continued to listen to Almighty describe His passion for me and how He longed for me to experience rest. We sat and talked for hours, and then something dawned on me. Almighty knew everything, and yet He was asking me questions as if He didn't know the answers. Why would He do that when He could read my thoughts? I was getting ready to leave, but knew if I didn't find the answer, I would be wrestling with this one for a while. I looked into His eyes. "Almighty, don't You know everything, and can't You even hear my thoughts?"

He looked at me intrigued, as if wondering where I was going with this. "You know I can."

"Well, then why…?"

"Why am I asking you questions that I already know the answers to?" He said, finishing my question.

"Yes," I responded quickly.

He was silent for several minutes while gazing at the night sky. Then He turned to me and spoke. "Did you ever think maybe I want you to verbalize things to me? I want you to tell me your deepest desires, the secret longings of your soul. I ask questions because I want to draw you out. Why do you think I tell you to pray, to ask me for what you need or desire? I already know what you need and what your desires are. I want you to know that you have asked me, and I have heard you. When you ask in faith, believing and knowing I've heard you, and knowing I will answer, it fills me with joy. It's a love language to me—you ask me for what you need, you depend on me. It gives me great pleasure."

"Really, just doing that one thing actually gives You pleasure?"

"Honestly, you can't comprehend how much satisfaction it gives me. When people don't trust me and choose to worry about things—jobs, marriages, what to eat and what to wear—it feels like a knife in my heart. They forget that I died for them, a brutal horrible death as a sin offering. I took care of the biggest problem they had, will ever have. For them to think that I can't handle the small things, or that I just don't care, or am not willing to help, is offensive. Helping—rescuing and saving—is my best quality. If I had a business card, it would read, "I am your Savior. I will redeem your life from destruction, and crown you with everlasting kindness and tender mercy. Call out to me. I am the only one who can give you real help.""

"You're everything I need, aren't you?"

"I AM"

His words sent chills through my entire body. This truth was the power that backed up everything else He had said.

After that night, I decided something. I would have faith in Almighty and live a life of rest. Now, not being worried and not being hurried isn't as easy as it sounds, but I strove for the rest He described. I took time to notice the world around me—the trees, and the flowers—to the point of throwing my worries into the cool, refreshing wind. Most of all, however, I spent time thinking about Almighty. The reality of His influence in my life brought the greatest rest.

More than just noticing the world around me, however, I watched something amazing happen, miraculous even. While enjoying this lifestyle of rest, my life began to pour out as a blessing to others more than it ever had while striving to do well. I did more good by accident than I ever did by intentionally trying. I noticed people. I had opportunities to help, and I acted on them. Almighty poured so much love into me, I couldn't contain it, and it flooded over onto others.

Out of His rest, I was energized and alive. I also poured massive amounts of grace on myself when confronted with my own failures and sins. When I did that, I found I was far more merciful to others than I'd ever been. The truth that Almighty was revealing to me had begun a change. It more than altered my mind, it rocked my entire world. By changing the way I thought and viewed life, it would change me? It changed the decisions I made. It changed my destiny.

As wonderful and freeing as these truths were that had been handed to me on a silver platter from the hand of Almighty, I began to have a greater desire for the One giving me these truths than the truths themselves. I felt He, Himself, was the truth, and that He, Himself, was the One setting me free, divinely and intricately unlocking the chains of my heart. My soul was stirred for Him.

The way He looked at me, the way He nurtured me with His eyes, somehow revealed to me that I was His greatest desire. He caused me to perceive it through the eyes of faith. I knew He agonized over me, protected me, and longingly watched me. I was His deepest passion, and now He was beginning to be mine.

I couldn't get Him out of my mind. He was a part of every thought, linked with everything I did. I couldn't separate myself from Him and didn't want to. I was comforted by His presence. In fact, the more severe the trial, the more extreme was the comfort. I felt that with Him I could go up against an army or scale a wall. Nothing was impossible if He was with me.

Things started to fall into slow motion. I felt as though every step, every movement was amplified. Poetry radiated from me in the daily mundane activities, just because Almighty was watching me. Everything became significant and beautiful, like abstract art. There was a whole world around Almighty I didn't understand. Cloaked in a tangible mystery, He was like no one else, and I wanted more than anything for that spark, that mystery, that fire to be inside me. I wanted to set the whole world aflame with the most valuable gift known to man.

CHAPTER 5

ADVERSARY'S ATTACK

"Who do you think you are?" an accusing voice cut through my thoughts.

"I'm Eppy," I responded.

"Yes, I know your name," Adversary retorted in a sarcastic tone, "but what business do you have linking so tightly with Almighty? Who do you think you *are*," he repeated. "Why do you think He wants to use you so powerfully? You are being ridiculous, you know that, right?"

I shook my head confidently, "He's given me promises of love and favor."

"Those aren't for you," he growled. "You're not worthy of those promises."

"I must agree with you on that point," I said. "I'm probably worse than you even know about."

At my words, Adversary released a blood-curdling scream. His eyes went from black to red and back to black. In a fit of rage, he began smashing my personal belongings. He tore up some of the things closest to my heart. I stood strong, solid. I would have fallen but felt Almighty holding me up with His hands.

All of the sudden, Adversary became silent, a strange eerie calm coming over him. His voice became deep, masculine, threatening. He rushed at me, backing me into a corner, trapped. Glaring into my eyes, he spoke in a slow steady tone. "I'm coming against you with all the forces of hell. There will be nowhere to run, nowhere to hide." He started to walk away but turned back and shot spiteful words at me. "You're a coward," he said, leaving that last word to hang in my thoughts.

I tried to blank out the long, steady stream of accusations, but some of the things he said shook me. There might be truth to the whole coward bit. The thought of him coming against me in battle with an army frightened me. I knew Almighty had immense amounts of power, but I had a suspicion that Adversary might have some power as well.

Several days went by. I let these thoughts run wild in my mind, breaking down protective barriers, opening doors and windows in the spirit realm, allowing fear to boldly enter and torment me. I was setting my mind on Adversary's negative lies and giving into fear. Almighty's words were shoved into second place in my mind. Maybe Adversary's points were valid. I knew Almighty forgave me completely and loved me deeply, but that didn't mean He would use me in powerful ways. Maybe the extremity of evil in my past and my heart did disqualify me for service. Like Adversary said, *who am I*?

As I was tossing these things to and fro in my mind, I heard a pounding on the door. Fear circled around me in a dance, chanting nefarious songs. The pounding grew louder. I froze. My mind went blank, my body weak and sallow. I had already disabled myself by listening to the lies for days.

In an instant, the door flew open to reveal a whole army of hellish imps led by Adversary. They grabbed me, put me in chains and dragged me off to a remote place in the wilderness. A grimy white cement building waited for me. I was taken down dark steps to a cold, damp basement and chained to the wall. This might have been tolerable if I were alone, but fear and oppression circled, taunting, jeering and speaking lies. Their words sucked the remainder of my strength.

Adversary entered the room, intent on talking some sense into me. "If Almighty is all about rest, then why are you in chains?" he said. "If you're so filled with His love, why don't you feel it now? And if He will never leave you, then why has He abandoned you?"

"He hasn't abandoned me," I whispered weakly, tears streaking down my cheeks. When I opened my mouth and spoke out those words, something odd happened. It was as though I had wounded Adversary.

For a moment, he cowered backward, as if he'd lost some of His power. Attempting to hide it, he continued to try to intimidate me. "You need to know something," he said in a malicious tone. "You're going to die. I am going to tear you apart at midnight and enjoy doing it. And since you deserve all this misery, and you know you do, there's no point in fighting it." He stared at me for several minutes with sadistic, horrifying eyes that caused fear to start dancing around me again.

I stared back at him. I detected fear in His eyes, hiding behind the evil. I wondered why he would experience fear while looking at me. I was chained to a wall. What was it in me that caused such alarm? After gazing at me with the intent of intimidation, he turned and stalked out, leaving me alone with my thoughts.

As I sat in the dark, damp cell, I remembered Almighty's words and the freedom He had brought to my heart. I needed Him. If I ended up in this dungeon by believing the words of Adversary, maybe I could get out by remembering the words of Almighty and thinking about Him. I remembered how He'd said all my righteousness was filthy rags, but He had clothed me with His righteousness. He said that He would stand by me and strengthen me and even though I walk through the valley of the shadow of death, I should fear no evil because He was with me. He promised to restore my soul and said He loved me with an everlasting love. I started to speak out these words at first in a whisper, then louder and louder until I was shouting. My faith gained strength!

I kept at this for several hours, but noticed I was still in chains. I also noticed something else. I didn't care. Then, peace began to overtake me. I started to sing songs of deliverance, songs of worship. I sang with grace in my heart toward the Lord. After singing for several more hours, I noticed I was *still* in chains, but I also noticed I *still* didn't care. Joy had overtaken me. I started laughing and singing louder and harder. I started professing my love for Almighty and meditating on His love for me.

Several days later, overwhelmed with exhaustion, I fell asleep in my chains. I was lying in sewage. I was sore from the cuts created by the iron cuffs around my wrists and ankles. But I got the best sleep of my life. I dreamed about Almighty taking me into His Kingdom and I felt His actual presence with me in my cell. When I awoke, my chains were loosed. The freedom I now felt on the inside far surpassed my concern of physically getting out of this prison.

A door had been cut in the wall, exposing a long hallway with a light at the other end. I followed it out and I was free. Green grass, pink and red flowers, trees and hills waited on the other side. I ran into the meadow and rolled in the grass laughing. I lay still, breathing in the meadow air, looking at the trees blowing in the wind and thinking about Almighty. As I lay there, looking at the sky, I saw Him standing over me. My heart pounded and I started to jump up to greet Him.

"Lay still," He said. So, I laid back and gazed up at Him. I felt such a deep, intense sense of adoration. I just wanted to lie there, looking up at Him, admiring His beauty and power forever. He stood over me for a while. One of the things that stirred me most was the loving expression on His face. I was the object of His affection. I delighted in looking at Him looking at me. I wanted nothing more than to lie at His feet for the rest of my life. Eventually, He bent down and lay beside me on the grass.

"I have a question," I said turning to Him.

"You always do," He said, smiling looking back at me.

"When I was locked in the cell and Adversary was badgering me, why did I see fear in His eyes? I was chained to the wall. He had full power."

Almighty turned to look at me and watched me for a while in silence. Finally, He spoke. "He saw me in your eyes and that terrified him. I have powers you haven't even remotely encountered. It's true Adversary could take you out apart from me, but you are never apart from me."

"Now I have a question for you," He said, "and it's something I've been wanting to ask you for a while."

"What is it?" I asked, wondering what question could be stirring in the vastness of Almighty's all-knowing mind.

"Why do you listen to Adversary?"

The question caught me off guard. I didn't have a good answer. Why did I? "I don't know why, I just go with the flow. Sometimes I'm not sure if it's Adversary or my own thoughts."

"Well, maybe you shouldn't listen to your own thoughts if they are going to lead you down dark roads into traps. You can't always just go with the flow when it comes to your thoughts. What you meditate on, you will believe. What you believe will end up manifesting itself through your actions."

"If I can't listen to Adversary and I can't even listen to myself, what's left?"

"Me, you have my words and my thoughts," He said.

"So, if I don't listen to Adversary and take my own thoughts out of the picture and only allow your words and thoughts in my head, I'd basically become a little version of you."

"Now, you're getting it," He said with a wink.

"That's what I want so badly, but it's not possible. I don't have control over my thoughts. I can't help what I think and feel."

"Who on this planet brainwashed you into thinking that? That's a straight-out formula for chaos and misery. People walk straight into sin because it feels right or because they've let their thoughts go there so often the action is inevitable. However, it *is* possible to capture damaging thoughts, put them in chains and annihilate them forever, or else there would be no hope for anyone.

"Regardless of what has happened to a person in his life, everyone has an extreme need for redemption. Without my grace, no one will make it. Any curse that has chained any person has been broken by me. I became a curse for everyone, but not everybody receives the freedom that's given. Many people choose to stay in chains.

"You have to go against the flow," He continued. "You have to deny yourself and what you ordinarily do, think or feel. It's hard at first—it may even feel impossible. If you've grown up feeling like a coward, then deny yourself and be bold as a lion. If you're tormented by guilt, you might have to preach the gospel to yourself every day. If you wrestle with feelings of worthlessness, remind yourself of the extraordinary value I have placed on you. You have to brainwash yourself with truth in order to un-brainwash yourself from all the lies. I am willing and able to reprogram a person's mind and change his life. Sadly, not everybody taps into my power or even knows how to. My words are power. My promises are power spoken out and received by faith."

CHAPTER 6

STIRRED UP

After Almighty confronted me on my interaction with Adversary, and the lies I had allowed to permeate my mind, I willfully began to think differently. When a lie would come in, I would counter it with a truth—always the words of Almighty. Lies couldn't stand up against truth. The lie would immediately be chained and dragged away to be executed.

For example, if I wanted to condemn myself for something seemingly legitimate, I reminded myself I couldn't be condemned for anything because I'm clothed in righteousness. If I felt alone, I remembered that He was always with me and had promised He would never leave me or forsake me. If I felt shame, I reminded myself I would never be put to shame because I was hidden in Almighty. And if I was tempted to willfully step into sin, I reminded myself of the stupidity and horrific repercussions of reaping what I sowed. I also reminded myself that Almighty wanted better of me because He loved me deeply.

Then I started practicing preemptive strikes. I began to fill my mind with truths before lies had a chance to enter. I thought about how He who knew no sin became sin for me that I might be the righteousness of God. As I thought about it, I could hardly believe it was true. It was too good to be true.

Another concept I couldn't even fathom,' He who was rich became poor that I through His poverty might become rich.' One thing I was starting to realize is the phrase, too good to be true, doesn't exist in Almighty's universe. I kept on with this practice and experienced joy and peace. I was able to speak truth into other people's lives, because I was so familiar with it. I was making myself more familiar with truths rather than lies.

In the midst of this tremendous victory, there was another stirring inside me. It was separate from right or wrong, but not necessarily separate from me and maybe not even from Almighty. It was the stirring up of desires. Desire was neither good nor bad in and of itself, but my desires were not directly linked with Almighty. I had personal passions. I was a visionary, but my visions began to intensify as well as my desire for them.

Sometimes, I thought I heard Adversary's voice in my head. He would switch from condemning me for having desires, to trying to push me into them at full intensity. At times, I didn't know which side was right, if any. I needed to ask Almighty. I sought Him as He had taught me. Sometimes He was there instantly, and sometimes the journey took me through forests where I looked behind every tree and through every meadow. Regardless, He always let Himself be found by me when I searched for Him with all my heart.

This time, He was deep in the heart of the darkest part of the woods, sitting on a rock and leaning against a tree. A bird rested on His hand. I thought I saw Him talking to it, but figured it was probably my imagination. As I got closer it was clear He was in fact talking to the bird.

"This is Petey," He said.

"Hi Petey, I'm Eppy" I said hesitantly. Petey squawked, cocked His head and then flew away.

"Did you just introduce me to a bird?"

"Yes," He said smiling at my confused expression.

"Oh. Is there a reason why?"

"I wanted you to see me interacting with the birds. I have great affection for them."

"Um, okay," I responded, but was anxious to get to the subject of importance. "I've been thinking about some things and…"

"Come to me," He said putting out His hand. "Come reason with me."

It had been a while since He had spoken those specific words to me. I was comforted by them. I put my hand in His and He pulled me onto the rock next to Him and put His arm around me. I was so focused on my questions, and on getting an answer, I was oblivious to the affection He was showing me.

"I have a lot of desires," I said getting right to the point.

"I do too," He said. "I can relate. And my biggest one is you."

I stared at Him. Was He even hearing me? It was as if He was in His own little romantic world.

"I know, I stuttered and… I'm glad. I just…want some things in this life."

"Like what?"

"Well, I have some things I'd like to do, you know, passions. Is it wrong?"

"Why on earth do you think it would be wrong to have desires?"

"Well, Adversary…" I began.

"Oh him" Almighty said. "I created you with longings. Everybody has specific things they're passionate about. And everybody is different, each having unique callings and gifts. You're supposed to follow your desires. It's likely I'm the one who placed them there. It's okay to have dreams."

Watching His face, I could see He was the biggest dreamer there was.

"I desire to give good gifts and to bring about a plan in your life greater than you could even dream up. The problem comes when people fix their eyes on their desires instead of me. The truth is none of those things will totally satisfy. The longer you know me, the more you will see that it's me you've truly desired all along, and I will become your vision in totality."

"So, it's okay to step out into what I want to do?" I asked, still not sure about the exact answer He was giving.

"Yes," He said objectively. "I made you to have longings you've never thought of. Are you willing to let me redirect you?"

My eyes dropped while I thought about my desires. I knew holding on too tightly was part of what Almighty meant about people fixing their eyes on their dreams instead of Him. "You can change my plans if you want to," I finally answered.

"Just know at the end of eternity, you will be absolutely overjoyed with any change I make." I felt Him gently caress my arm. "I like the birds," He said, "but I care so much more about what happens to you than the birds."

It was an interesting comparison. The birds were simple creatures. They just flew around, made their nests and ate their worms. They didn't seem to worry about much. Oh, and apparently, they liked talking to Almighty. I wondered why people worry. Why did I worry?

"Your desires are important to me," He continued. "Animals of the earth are not able to think or reason. They are driven by instinct. Thinking is an ability I have only given to humans. You are made in my image. I wouldn't just send you down here without a path, without a purpose, to wander around aimlessly." He caught my eyes. "The deepest, most mysterious, almost unknown and unrecognized desire in the core of mankind is the desire for me. Once realized, it causes all other longings to be intertwined with me."

I tilted my head, thinking. I still didn't know how one Being could have total preeminence in a person's life, but I thought about how Almighty always brought everything back to Himself. He is the cure, He is salvation, He is my answer, He is my security, He is my hope, He is my desire. He is the past, the present, and the future. When He reminded me of this, it was always oddly refreshing, relieving the burden of myself. He took on all the responsibility for my existence from beginning to the end!

And then, the moment of freedom passed, and I went back to thinking about myself apart from Him—my plans, my hopes, my dreams. I wondered at my propensity to do this. Almighty continued to sit beside me in silence, enjoying the moment, enjoying my presence. Then, as the sky began to turn dark, I decided to go home. Without a word, I stood to leave.

As I moved away, Almighty grabbed my hand and pulled me toward Himself. He lowered His head and kissed my hand. Lifting His head, He looked into my eyes. "Remember me," He said.

I stood there for a moment with my hand in His, looking at Him. Without a reply, I turned and walked away. After I got several yards away, I turned back and saw He had another bird resting on His hand. He glanced at me, gave me a wink and then looked back at the bird and continued talking to it.

I went home that day, continued with my life and became more and more focused on what I wanted. One part of me wanted to stay near Almighty completely, but that was a part of me I protected, a vulnerable part. It was a part of me I didn't fully know, a part I kept hidden and covered. It lurked as a secret place that I only visited when it was absolutely necessary, as when tragedy hit, or I had a question I couldn't comprehend, or when severe oppression overtook me.

When I was with Him, I was at rest—open, exposed, forced to see truth—but at rest and set free. When alone, however, I was in a comfortable battleground, a familiar prison, so I slid back into self. I stayed there for a while, but every so often, the last words Almighty had spoken to me would come back into my mind. Remember me. Remember me. In those moments, I did, but then my thoughts would move along to the next thing I was preoccupied with, and I willfully and quickly forgot.

Then something happened that interrupted the monotony. Every day, as soon as I opened my door to start down the path before me, I noticed Almighty in the distance. He was kneeling, praying intensely. What was He praying for? I did not know. I ignored it day after day and continued on my journey into the city. Each day that went by, each day that I ignored it, His praying became more intense. Several times, I even saw Him weeping. He was praying out loud, but He was using a language that was foreign to me. Then, He was gone. I continued on with my life, but a subtle feeling of emptiness had crept into my soul. I needed something more. Dissatisfaction had taken over.

One day as I opened my door, I saw Almighty sitting under a tree in front of my house. He was clearly waiting for me. When I came out, He stood up and held out His hand.

"Where are we going," I asked. I wanted to know before committing to putting my hand in His.

"I want to show you something," He said, not giving me the response I was looking for.

"Where are we going?" I insisted still not giving Him my hand.

"It's a surprise," He said.

"I don't like surprises," I said committed to my stubbornness.

His eyes cut into me. He studied me for a while still holding out His hand. "Do you trust me?" He asked, getting right to the heart of the issue.

I didn't answer, but defiantly looked in the other direction.

"If you trust me," He continued, "you'll take my hand and follow me without knowing where we are going, how we're going to get there, and what's on the other end. You' would be happy to take this walk with me, just for the time we are together. Can't you ever anticipate the best of me when we're walking out into the unknown?" His words jarred me. "I know you've suffered pain at the hands of Adversary and at the hands of yourself, but how long will this self-protection go on when it comes to me, your Redeemer?"

His words forced my hand into His and He closed His hand around mine. He didn't seem to care how or why I had put my hand into His, just as long as He was holding my hand and leading me to some new, random, unknown place. He referred to this as "adventure" and "walking by faith."

He led me down some familiar paths, but with unfamiliar trees and streams. The streams that were once a trickle had turned into a gently flowing river. The unique trees I didn't recognize began to turn into fruit trees. Then, the river became a solid body of water, fruit trees lining the banks.

"This is where we stop," He said, bringing me to the water's edge underneath a bizarre-looking fruit tree. He reached up and pulled off a pink-colored fruit from the tree that covered us like a canopy. "Try this," He said, handing me the fruit.

"No thank you," I responded and pushed His hand away.

"You'll like it," He said.

"I don't want it," I snapped.

"Its sweet nourishment," He persisted.

"I don't need it," I said stubbornly.

He smiled at me and pulled it away. He looked at me as if He was in love, delighting in me with His eyes. His whole face filled with amusement and wonder. He knelt down and picked up a baseball-sized rock. Placing the fruit on the ground, He smashed it open with the rock and began to eat from the pieces. As He ate, the fruit stirred an awakening in His body that I could visibly see new life coursing through His veins.

After eating half of the fruit, He took the remainder of the pieces and squeezed them, then rubbed the juice over His skin. I didn't ask why He did this, content with watching in silence. Next, He did one final act. He picked some leaves off the fruit tree and crushed them between two rocks. He took the oil from the leaves and anointed His head with it. He gazed at me. "I want to do the same things to you that I am doing to myself. Will you let me?" He asked.

I looked at Him, not knowing how to answer the question. "Maybe someday," I said.

"Alright," He said, content with my response. He leaned against the fruit tree and closed His eyes.

I stared at Him for a while, wondering what He was going to do next. I wondered what all this meant. Almighty would show me little snippets of things, but not the whole picture. I wanted to know what He was up to, but He didn't care much about giving me that information. I could tell that all He wanted to do was sit there and enjoy the moment with me.

I sat down next to Him, both of us silent. Almighty usually initiated our conversations, often by planting a thought or question in my mind, but He didn't this time. I started to realize it was because something was off. There was something simmering in His soul underneath the surface. I decided not to delve into the issue at all, but to leave. I stood up and started to walk away.

"Eppy," Almighty said in a soft, but serious voice.

I ignored Him and kept walking, not even glancing back.

"Will you not ever stir yourself up to take hold of me?"

I froze. His words cut into me like millions of microscopic daggers sending an ache into the deepest part of my being. I spun around to look at Him, but He was gone.

"Almighty," I called out, but He didn't respond. How did I get to this apathetic state? It had crept up on me like an early autumn chill. I ran out of the woods, away from the creek, away from the trees and back to my familiar territory. But I had no rest. All I could think about were those words. Will you not ever stir yourself up to take hold of me? Those words haunted me.

I finally fell asleep, only to awake in the middle of the night in a cold sweat. Multiple images flashed through my mind. I remembered how Almighty had rescued me from the cabin Adversary had seduced me into. I remembered how Almighty had put me over His shoulder and set me on His horse, where we had ridden away to the unknown. I thought about how He laid my head on His chest, causing me to hear

His heartbeat. I thought about His wild, unrelenting passion for me and His obsessive, detailed awareness of me.

Images of the cross asserted themselves in my mind—brutal, indescribable, His flesh stripped from His body, unrecognized as human, His soul oppressed. He had hung naked on the cross—He, a spotless, perfect creature, wild and untamed, beautiful and powerful, willingly driven to this sacrifice by love. My heart began to burn within me. Hot tears fell over my face.

I slumped to the floor and cried so loud that I felt my spirit begin to awake from its hibernation. I kicked open the door and ran out into the cold, dark, rainy night, sobbing. I ran and ran, hard and fast, with passion and purpose. "Almighty, Almighty," I yelled out through tears. I kept running and screaming out His name at the top of my lungs. "Almighty!" Finally, I collapsed, exhausted, cold, wet and dehydrated. I curled up into a ball in the dirt, yearning for Almighty's presence. Icy tears fell to the ground. I shivered, my body aching. I kept whispering His name.

Then He was there standing before me, looking down at me with sweet compassion in His eyes.

I jumped up and clung to His waist, crying against him. "I love you so much, need you so much."

His arms closed around me and locked me to Him. Rest ran through my body, yet I started shaking from the cold and the emotional experience of the night. Almighty took off His overcoat and wrapped it around me, leaving Himself exposed to the icy elements. He seemed unfazed by this. His whole world revolved around me.

So, why then shouldn't my whole world revolve around Him? That would make everything perfect, harmonious. Whenever I let Him into my heart, when I took down all my barriers, joy and peace coursed through me. Still, I kept running away, I kept building walls, and I kept going to sleep. Yet, He kept awakening me.

"Eppy," Almighty whispered, still sheltering me tightly in His arms. "My mercies are new every morning."

I felt the tears start to flow again as He spoke these words. Almighty always had a solution, an answer, a way to show kindness to me. It was as if nothing could get past Him. I couldn't get away from Him. I didn't want to. I was being unrelentingly chased by His grace. I bowed before Him and worshiped, still clothed in His warm robe. My heart filled with the warmth of His love. When I worshiped Him, I felt the burden of self lifting off me. I was overshadowed by Him, safe in His sovereign hand. I became light as air when the heaviness of self was given up to Almighty. I was free.

Then, I wondered, Who am I that He would do this for me? Who am I that He would take my burdens away and take them on Himself? I am an ungrateful wretch. Most of the time I don't even acknowledge Him, and yet He gave up glory for me and went to hell on my behalf. And now, He tells me His mercy is new every day, which upon reflection is probably the regular dose of mercy that I need. "I don't want to be significant," I exclaimed, still prostrate at His feet. "I don't want to be anything. I just want to lay at your feet forever. This is where I am the happiest. This is where I am the freest."

Almighty was elated. I didn't need to see the expression on His face, because I felt new levels of ecstasy pour over me until my entire body was tingling. It wasn't an emotion that gave me this experience, it was truth and truth alone. I knew that He was all I wanted in this life. My heart confirmed that to me in this moment. Everything else given or experienced would have to be deeply saturated in Him or it would be meaningless, something I didn't want any part of. Almighty gave everything its flavor, its life. I was so in love. All of my senses were heightened. I began to kiss His feet that still bore scars of the nail driven through them. I traced my fingers over the holes. Why, I began to ask myself. Why?

Almighty answered me in a whisper. "Crazy love will take you right to a cross."

A song burst from my lips, strong and loud. When I finished singing, I began to kiss His feet again. I thought about the woman who washed His feet with her tears and dried them with her hair. I identified with her. She was an immoral woman, rejected by everyone else in her day. Lost, alone, rebellious, but in love. I stood up and wrapped my arms around His waist again. "Whatever you want from me, I will do," I said. "I'm yours, just tell me what you want."

Almighty smiled down at me, stroking my hair with one hand and holding my head with the other. "I want you to know me," He said. "To know the power of my resurrection and the fellowship of my sufferings, being conformed to my death that you too might obtain resurrection from the dead."

I didn't totally understand what He meant by everything He said, but I kept thinking about the words, I want you to know me. He didn't want me to do anything or accomplish anything, He just wanted me to know Him! Actually, when I thought about it, He had been trying to get this message across to me for a while now. The power of His resurrection and the fellowship of His suffering, I would have to think about these words. Most of what Almighty said went over my head, but His love for me was extreme, regardless of what I did or didn't understand.

He cradled my head on His chest for a few hours. He didn't want to move and neither did I. He just held me close to Himself. I allowed my mind to go blank. I freed myself from thinking, striving or trying to understand anything that didn't involve this intimate moment with Almighty. We just delighted in each other.

Then, finally, Almighty lifted my head and looked into my eyes. "You need some friends. You're a loner. I want you to get into fellowship."

"I like being alone," I resisted.

"You need people, Eppy."

"I don't like people," I persisted. "They're horrible."

"People are people. They're human like you. You scrape against and sharpen each other, as iron sharpening iron."

"It sounds painful."

"It is, He said honestly. "I want you to get into a fellowship and love people like I love them, laying your life down for your friends. You must become vulnerable and humble, and esteem others better than yourself. It's going to put you to death but make you alive."

I didn't like where Almighty was going with this, not one bit. For me to motivate myself into real meaningful interactions with other people—interactions that would cause me to tear down my walls—would be a real challenge. Sighing, I realized it would be easier to take my mind and emotions out of the picture and by faith just do what Almighty told me to do.

"I know you are guarded," Almighty continued. "But I'm going to do everything in my power to take your guard down and remove any final barriers that keep you from total, unadulterated freedom."

"I know your intentions are good," I said timidly. "But do you even know how insecure and crazy people are? They're evil and they make up things."

"You should look in the mirror sometime," Almighty said with a playful smirk on His face.

I know He wanted more for me than to just get to know a few people and create surface interaction with them. He wanted me to pour out my soul—expose my deepest fears and failures, and willingly let them have the upper hand in the relationship. This was going to be terrifying. Yet, when I reconciled myself to obedience, peace came over me. One thing I knew for sure, Almighty was mad about me. I found myself wondering why I wouldn't trust this crazy love that would take Him to a cross.

"Just enjoy the moment with me," Almighty said. He pulled me down to sit beside Him as we watched the sun go down. I remembered doing this with Him once before. The beauty of the night sky spoke of Him. It exuded a glory that mirrored His personality exactly. The purple, orange, and pink of the sunset was breathtaking like Almighty. It was refreshing being so close to Him and allowing Him to love me. He was always wise and always right.

***

In the days that followed, I thought I would give people a try. It couldn't hurt. It seemed important to Almighty that I make friends. I started attending a church and people welcomed me with open arms in the beginning. It was amazing to be able to talk to people who shared a mutual love for Almighty with me. It gave me encouragement and hope. I began bonding with people I had only known a short time. I began to lose sight of myself and focus on the needs of those around me.

However, when I got comfortable enough to open up about my past, everything changed. It was a very subtle, but very real change. Everyone was still friendly when I was at church, but they didn't want to spend time with me alone. They didn't invite me to join them when they went out together in groups. I began to taste the bitterness of hypocrisy and self-righteousness. I realized something. People are not nearly as merciful as Almighty. They all seemed to appreciate Him and have affection for Him, so I half expected them to be like Him. But to be honest, they were more like me.

I had a problem. I had opened myself up to people enough to realize I needed them. I couldn't run away, but I had experienced hurt and frustration as a result of my honesty. I closed my eyes and thought about my sensitive dilemma. What would Almighty do? Would He suck it up and just take the passive abuse or would He take out His whip? Perhaps there was another alternative.

I soon experienced an incident where I was the brunt of vicious gossip. I found out through the grapevine, so I decided to leave the church for a while. Things just weren't right. It angered me.

After I distanced myself from others, Adversary began making periodic visits to talk the situation over with me. I tried to resist Him, but I was already so confused I almost wanted to hear what He had to say.

"Don't you think it was a little unfair of Almighty to push you to make friends knowing how they would treat you? He knows all things so why would He do that?"

"He must have had a good reason," I said defensively. "I know He cares a lot about me."

"Does he?" Adversary snapped back.

"There is no way you can get me to question Almighty's love for me. I'm not even going to let you plant that seed in my mind," I said, raising my voice louder than I even realized.

"Eppy," Adversary said sharply. "Let's look at the facts, shall we? Almighty practically pushes you into fellowship, He lets you take your guard down, and those people abuse you. Don't you have any self-worth? Something is wrong with the churches today. You need to rise up and take a stand for righteousness. This whole trusting Almighty thing is getting very old. When are you going to see results? When are you going to have victory? Is He just going to leave you in the dark forever? Does He regard you like an insect on a wall? Do you think it's attractive to just take abuse?"

"But I can't please Almighty without faith. It's impossible," I protested.

"Oh, so now your whole purpose in life is just to please Almighty. Is that it? You're just going to put all your eggs in His loony idiotic basket? You're growing affection for Him is making me sick. You need to think for yourself. You're not being realistic. You have your head in the clouds, and all this talk about faith is making me very uncomfortable. I have known Him a lot longer than you have. He just lets garbage happen to people. I've seen it time and time again. Don't be naive. Are you sure you want to trust Him the way you trusted those people at church?"

Adversary was beginning to build a case. I knew I needed to have faith, but that sounded like a weak answer. "Just go away. I've heard enough," I said.

"Remember what I said," he reiterated as he left.

I knew I had hit a crossroad with understanding Almighty's nature. It seemed that bad things did happen to people, and it seemed that it was often allowed by Almighty. But Almighty had put too much trust in my heart for me to just walk away. I wrestled with these things continually. It was more than just the experiences that had happened to me, now I was thinking in a wider scope. Suffering saturated the planet—on the innocent, not just the guilty. What about rape, murder and abuse?

What about me? I was horrible. I hurt many innocent people. I was aware I'd never fully understood Almighty, but this was a new level of mystery that plagued me. As a result of these experiences at church and my recent dialogue with Adversary, I not only avoided people, but I also avoided Almighty. I crawled into a dark hole of misery, my anxious thoughts, stuck on the terrors of life, were my only companions. I began to see how my thinking led me to my current reality. All the situations that I'd found myself in began with a thought—or lack of thought in some cases. These issues were troubling, yet the spark of faith had not diminished in my heart.

Wherever I went, I began to notice Almighty in the distance, praying. It was a regular thing. I couldn't get away from Him. One morning, He was in my yard, not praying, but sitting on the ground, looking up at the sky. As soon as I looked at Him, He turned His head toward me and locked eyes with me. As He looked at me, I almost wanted to cry. "Come to me," He said.

His eyes drew me in. I had to obey. I walked toward Him. When I reached Him, He grabbed my hand and pulled me down onto His lap. He had never done this before. I started shaking. He closed His arms around me and held me securely. Then the tears came. I cried so loudly it was as if I was releasing all of my pain from childhood until the present. He didn't speak and I didn't speak. I just felt His arms around me and allowed the silence and His presence to bring cleansing to my heart.

"My Eppy," He finally said. "I've missed you." He wiped the tears from my face and looked at me. "I know you have questions," He said softly, almost in a whisper.

I was quiet for a moment, and then I let it all out. "I just don't understand why you let those people treat me that way with their subtle self-righteousness and demeaning gossip. They rejected me. They totally withdrew their friendship from me. They acted like I was on a completely different level than them."

Almighty was smiling at me as I spoke. In times past, this would have bothered me, but I knew Him enough to know He wasn't trying to be demeaning. He just delighted in me all the time, no matter what I did or said.

"Let me tell you something, Eppy. Arrogant, self-righteous pride is the thing I hate the most. I loathe it from the deepest part of my soul. You are a part of me. If they take a swing at you, they are taking a swing at me. Real love has to be humble, or it's not love at all. Love identifies with the person. I identified with the darkest, most loathsome sins of humanity when I went to the cross. I stood outside the camp with the outcasts and sinners. I wanted to be there because I have such a love for them. I was considered a bastard, was mocked by the religious system of my day.

"Sinners, and those rejected by society and religiosity, flocked to me. They found rest in me, comfort instead of condemnation. I gave them acceptance and hope for redemption. I identified with them to such a degree the religious leaders rejected me though I did nothing wrong. I didn't come for those who think they're healthy, I came for those who know they're sick. The world is dark and full of evil, but I came to redeem, not to condemn those in it. Through me, the world is saved. It doesn't matter if someone is a victim of rape or the rapist. My arms are open wide. If anyone comes to me, I will in no way cast him away, but I will receive him as my own, and I will love him like no one ever has."

"So, what about all those hypocrites I became friends with? They seemed to know you but turned on me!"

Almighty grew silent, looking off into the distance for a moment, then turning His eyes back toward me He said. "I want you to go back to that church and I want you to love them like I would."

"What? You just said you hate the way they were acting. You said self-righteous pride is the thing that you hate the most."

"I still love them, and I want you to be an example of my love. After a short time, I am going to remove you from that group of people and bring you into a body of believers that have a great understanding of and love for my grace. In this group, you will have true fellowship and times of refreshing will come to you from me. However, sometimes you will need humility before people who think they're better than you. Willfully surrendering is the only way to truly be like me."

"How is that even possible Almighty? It's so humiliating, how can I have that much love?"

He looked at me, smiling again. "By thinking about me, and how much I am in love with you," He said. "That will give you strength. Just know I have your back, and I always will."

"I think they are better than me, Almighty."

"What do you mean, Eppy?"

"Well, I did some pretty sick things. I mean, how can you not think that a person who lived a pure, good life is better than me?"

"Eppy," Almighty said, His voice filled with passion, "They may have made wiser choices than you and avoided some of the painful repercussions of sin, but they are just as depraved in their deceitful, desperately wicked hearts. No one is righteous, not one. All people need to realize they are worse than what they most despise. The fury of my sovereign eyes will sear through their empty pride. I hate sin. It hurts people. It puts people in bondage and misery. So, I took it upon myself to become a man and absorb my own wrath, in order to give humanity a way of escape."

"Alright, I will go back and show them love." It wasn't a flippant decision. What could I say to Him? He was right.

Almighty was still holding me on His lap and as I agreed to go back, He pulled me close to Himself and held me tightly. He held me so tight and for so long, I thought He wasn't going to let go. Finally, He reluctantly released me. "I love you," He said as I stood up to leave.

"I know," I replied confidently and started to walk away. Then, I turned and asked, "You've been praying a lot. Is everything ok?"

"I've been praying for you, I always pray for you."

"Oh, how long have you been doing that for me?"

"Before you were thought into existence," He said. "I live to make intercession for you."

I stood staring at Him for a while, not comprehending His devotion to me. As I walked away, I thought about the intensity with which He'd been praying, sometimes even sobbing. His love was a mystery I might never solve.

So, I went to the church and rejoined fellowship with the people who had turned on me. It was hard as heck. It was especially hard because it was so subtle. People seemingly welcomed me back with open arms, but I could see in their faces that they were imagining what I had done when I was gone. Almighty once told me that He looks on the heart, but I knew with absolute certainty that people are not that way. No matter how loving they appear, they look on the outward appearance. This stirred a powerful desire in me to resist this behavior. I wanted so much to be like Almighty, to love recklessly and relentlessly, even at the expense of my own skin.

After I returned with this mentality and purpose in my heart, several things happened. First, there was a separation. When I took my guard down and gave genuine time and attention to people, half became cold and cynical and the other half, I think, actually became genuine. A change took place in their hearts. When I manifested my kindness and humility toward them, they became ashamed of their gossip. The cold and cynical group avoided me as if they were afraid of me. I didn't know I had the capacity to affect people so powerfully through transparency and humility. It was a complete and total revelation.

The next thing that happened was I began to notice the outcast, the person who was a little different. The one you were nice to, but certainly wouldn't be buddy-buddy with, and definitely wouldn't want to identify with. I flocked to those people and gave them refuge by extending my hand and attention. I saw Almighty's hand in it. It was all being orchestrated by Him. He had brought me here to show that good silences evil doers.

There were so many lessons in this that I was afraid I was going to miss one. All of the hurt was more than worth the revelation. Sometimes victory comes from defeat, exultation comes from humiliation and life comes from death. It's hard and challenging, with many ups and downs, but it was worth it.

After my season there was up, Almighty did as He had promised. He brought me into a new fellowship. This group of believers was different. They were unlike anything I'd ever known. There was such a spirit of unity and loving-kindness and joy, it was almost tangible. People actually delighted in each other. There was no jealousy or backbiting. It wasn't a popularity contest. The cross made everyone equal.

When someone mourned, everyone mourned with them as if they were broken hearted. When someone rejoiced, everyone rejoiced as if they were the one receiving the victory or getting the blessings poured out. People actually seemed happier when something good happened to their brother or sister than if something wonderful happened to them. The spirit of Almighty swept through the place. There was excitement, joy, singing and dancing. There was anticipation of Almighty's goodness, and faith to receive His blessings and pour them back out. As soon as something was given, it was released. They worshiped Him in the beauty of His holiness, and everyone esteemed each other better than themselves.

If I could boil everything down to one word, it would be freedom. I knew that freedom came from the spirit of Almighty walking in and around the sanctuary. Even the leaders saw themselves as no better than anyone else. They scoffed at anyone who put them up on any kind of weird pedestal, which unfortunately I started to do. I saw the glory and the grace in certain specific people, and I began to esteem them so high that I almost forgot they were human. I somehow thought they were exempt from fault and sin. I knew these growing thoughts weren't good for my soul.

One night I heard Almighty's voice waking me from my sleep. "Eppy," He called out in a non-audible, but just as real voice. "Not many mighty or noble have I called, but I have chosen the foolish things of this world to confound the wise, and the base things to confuse the great. The leaders you esteem so highly are base and utterly foolish. I chose them, poured my grace upon them, and love them very much, but they are people just like you, no better no worse."

That was all Almighty needed to say, and it immediately set things straight for me because I began to think about myself. I realized that He had chosen me, and I was most definitely depraved. It was actually unfair of me to put those people on a pedestal because when I saw their humanity, they would fall off the pedestal fast and hard. They were merely examples of His grace, like me.

I continued in my fellowship and let it bring me to new heights and new levels of understanding.

CHAPTER 7

I AM COMING UPON YOU

I began to sense a change in season, not just physically, but spiritually as well. I heard it in the wind and felt it in my bones. The lush green meadows became dry empty deserts. The beautiful canopy of trees became shriveled up dead sticks, and the rivers and streams now were waterless crevices. But even worse than the forest becoming a wilderness, I couldn't find Almighty. He was missing. I searched behind every tree in every field—all the usual places, plus many places that were not usual. It started okay. I got by for a little while. I had fellowship, had my routine and tried to forget He was gone, but it soon became unbearable, and I felt the sting of solitude.

I choked on the dust, my spirit parched. I craved the water of hearing His voice and being in His presence. Sometimes I would go on a long, detailed search, and then I would reconcile myself to loneliness. Then, I would get frustrated again and dart out into the wilderness screaming out Almighty's name. Sometimes I just broke down and cried. I wondered if He would ever come back, but deep down inside I believed He would. So, I waited and waited.

One evening, I wandered out to where our meadow had been. It was now a desert wasteland. I went up to the tree that we had once sat under, which was now leafless and looked like it had been dead a hundred years. I curled up under the tree and imagined Almighty cradling me in His arms. The evening became night. The stars shone through the clear night sky. I fell fast asleep and Almighty visited me in a dream.

"I know you've been searching for me," He said. "You've looked north and south but could not find me. You've gone east and west, and I was concealed. But Eppy, I know where you are going and when I've tested you, you will come forth as gold."

I awoke as the sun was rising and pondered the vision. I was comforted by Almighty's voice in the dream, but when I thought about His words, I grew frustrated. He knew I was looking for Him. He knew I felt alone and yet He intentionally hid Himself from me. Why would He do that? It almost seemed unlike Him. I wanted to hold onto faith like the other times I had been troubled and confused, but it was hard when there was nothing to latch onto. I had put all my hope in Almighty. He taught me that He is the only true hope and source.

So, I let go of my affection for other things that might have had a hold on me. Almighty was the only one that truly captivated my heart. I was completely at this mercy. I actually enjoyed this since He was so good and so completely in love with me. But it was hard to trust Him right now when He was so far away. And in these troubled times, Adversary was becoming an all too-familiar friend.

Almighty had once told me that faith is the substance of things hoped for and the evidence of things not seen, but how can having mere hope in something be substance and the invisible be evidence? The very definition of the word faith required faith to believe it. It was so allusive, so intangible. I guess through faith we cross a barrier to the unseen world, to the unseen beings into the very throne room of Almighty. Almighty also once said faith was a kind of love language for Him, bringing Him great pleasure.

If Almighty was testing my faith or trying to build my faith or whatever, He doesn't need to. I already have enough, I thought to myself. Since He had given me a clue as to the nature of the circumstance, I decided to stop looking for Him and just wait it out. Months went by, and time seemed to mock me.

Finally, one morning, I heard Him calling me. It was dawn, and He woke me from my sleep as the sun was rising. "Eppy," He said softly.

"Where have you been, I demanded? I needed you and you just took off and went on vacation somewhere. Why didn't you come when I called?"

"Do you know why I named you Eppy?" He asked, changing the subject and ignoring my questions.

"My mother named me Eppy," I snapped.

"Who do you think put the idea in her mind?"

"Ok why did you name me that," I said, growing more annoyed and frustrated with each passing second.

"Eppy is short for eppinosis, which means coming upon. I am sending my Spirit upon you. You will heal the sick, bind up the broken hearted, set the captives free, and you will prophesy. My word will be a flame of fire on your tongue. My Spirit will pour through you and out of you will come torrents of living water."

"Almighty, where have you been?" I persisted.

"Eppy, don't you know by now that I love you. I didn't go on vacation. I've been with you the entire time, watching, protecting, and listening to you. Do you really think for one moment I would take my eyes off you? Everything I do is in your best interest."

"So, You not being around was in my best interest?"

"I was around, but because you didn't experience My presence in the same way, you had to exercise more faith than usual. I promised I would never leave you or forsake you, and I never have and never will. Now allow me to repeat what I just said because obviously you weren't listening. I am sending my Spirit upon you. You will heal the sick, bind up the broken hearted, set the captives free and you will prophesy. My word will be a flame of fire on your tongue. My Spirit will pour through you and out of you will come torrents of living water."

"I can't do any of that stuff."

"I know, I'm going to do it through you," He answered.

"But I can't do it even if you're doing it through me."

Almighty laughed. "Eppy, sometimes you really don't know what you are talking about."

My mind started to race. There was no way I could prophesy. And heal a sick person? I didn't even know if I wanted to do that. Why couldn't Almighty just do it Himself? Why did He have to involve me? I didn't have a lot of compassion for people.

"Eppy, my using you is a gift to you, a blessing. You will receive back so much more than you give out."

"This is too much. Find someone else. I am weak, definitely lacking charisma and confidence. Not to mention, my sick past and my hard heart. You're really bad at choosing a good candidate for ministry."

"Listen to me," He said in a scolding tone, interrupting my arguments. "First of all, your past is covered by my blood. I see you as righteous, perfect and pure. Secondly, your hard heart is gone because I have given you a new heart. I have removed your heart of stone and given you a heart of flesh. It's true the heart is deceitful and desperately wicked, but even when your heart condemns you, I am greater than your heart and know all things. And finally, let's discuss this whole concept of weakness," He said, laughing again. "I only use the weak. Either I find a weak person, or I make a weak person through a breaking process. So be thankful you are already there. Weakness isn't a problem, it's a prerequisite."

"Almighty, how is this going to happen? I've been wondering around in the wilderness for months and it feels like years. I've been aimless and dry, directionless and frustrated. I would be the blind leading the blind. I'm surrounded by desert, so how can I give out water?"

"I know you love me," He said in a gentle voice. "You love me because I first loved you."

I felt pools of water well up in my eyes. He was right, despite my arguing and my contentious nature, I had a passion for Him that I couldn't quench. It had all started with Him. His love for me sparked the fire that was now burning inside my heart.

"Let me tell you a story. There was once a girl who spent time in the desert. In fact, she'd driven on a desert road to the middle of nowhere, with the city far behind. Her car ran out of gas, and she wondered what she was doing there. She stepped out of her car and searched the wilderness around her, feeling lost and alone, not even sure how she got there."

As I was listening to Almighty describe the condition of my spirit, I was amazed at the accuracy of this picture He created. I was also uncomfortable with the fact He knew me better than I knew myself.

"She grew frustrated," He continued. "She cried out to me, but all she could hear was the echoing of her own voice. She knew she was lost, knew she was in the wilderness, and believed she was alone. But there was something she didn't know. She had left a trail of gasoline all the way back to the city. That trail is her love for me, the passion I placed inside her. I'm going to spark that trail of fluid and light a fire all the way back to the city.

"You know I'm talking about you, Eppy. Everywhere you are, everywhere you've been, and everywhere you're going has purpose. You had no idea you left a gasoline trail. All you knew was you were lost in the wilderness alone. Trust what I see, not what you see, what I know, not what you know, what I understand, not what you understand. I am going to do a work in you that you wouldn't believe even if it were told to you."

That was the last thing Almighty said that day before leaving me alone with my thoughts. All this talk about fire and prophecy and healing the broken hearted made me nervous. It was uncharted territory. I didn't associate any of those things with myself. By the end of the day, I was exhausted from thinking about all these things. I finally decided if Almighty said He was going to do something in me and through me, He would do it. I didn't even need to worry because He would make it happen.

A week later, almost to the exact hour of when I had finished my conversation with Almighty, I found myself on a train heading north. I was seated next to a pimp named Sam. He revealed his identity to me because he tried to recruit me. It was a strange conversation. I kept envisioning him as a little boy, a wounded child. I shared some of my past, some of the things I did, some of the things that happened to me. I told him how Almighty had pulled me out of darkness and had given me a reason to hope, my entire reason for living. I couldn't help talking about Almighty, I was so proud that He loved me.

Then oddly enough, Sam opened up about his childhood. He had been molested by his stepdad for ten years. His mother actually knew about it and allowed it to continue because of her affection for the man. When Sam was a teenager, he got entangled with homosexuality and was ridiculed by people in his high school. He became an outcast on the verge of suicide, so he dropped out of high school and ran away to the nearest city. It was no better there. He was abused again when a stranger found him, took him in, made him a pimp, forcing him to work the streets. By the time I met Sam, he'd been a pimp for fifteen years.

As I listened to him, I thought if he were to meet Almighty, maybe Sam would be helped too. I grew excited about all the possibilities of a new life for this man. My mind went wild, my heart aching for him, knowing how it felt to be on the other side of redemption.

"Is Almighty the reason for the hope I see in you?" Sam asked.

I smiled. "Yes. He is all my reasons. All my hopes are wrapped up in His kindness toward me. I have never been disappointed yet."

Sam lowered His head, shame washing over his face. "Do you think Almighty would consider meeting with a wicked wretch like me?"

"You are the kind of person Almighty is attracted to," I said grinning, almost laughing.

"If He's so good and perfect, why would He be attracted to me? I'm confused about this guy."

"At first, I was too because He's so unique. It takes years to understand Him and even then, you are just scratching the surface of a universe with infinite layers. You are His favorite kind of person because you realize you need His help. Really, everybody needs His help, just not everyone realizes it."

Sam chewed his lip. "You really think He would help me?"

"I know He would," I said confidently. "Helping people is His favorite thing to do. And because I know Him, I can tell you there are things you will discover about Him that will surprise you. I don't want to bring up the word love too early, but there's a fire in His soul that burns with passion. Once tapped into, it releases power, and it will satisfy the deepest longings in your being. His love can heal your hurts, relieve your anger and free your guilt."

Sam sat across from me. Tears began to course down his cheeks, then sobs shook him with such intensity I didn't think he was breathing. "I want it, I want it," he pleaded.

"All right," I said, putting my hand on his back. "I will take you to Him."

I spent the next few weeks taking people to Almighty. My eyes opened to the world around me. Somehow, people just came into my path. I witnessed as person after person was set free and delivered. All I had to do was introduce them to Almighty and He took care of them. It was like bringing them to the hospital.

There was one lady I found living under a bridge. I later discovered she was strung out on a whole plethora of drugs. I had set out on a walk at dusk, compelled by my spirit to do so, and I heard her screaming out nonsensical phrases. She was paranoid and talking in parables. I rushed under the bridge to see what the commotion was. As I drew near, I watched her scream and cry, cutting herself with sharp rocks from the creek. As I studied her, I was hit with a terrifying thought— this was me I was looking at. This is where I would be, had Almighty not found me and rescued me when He did. I would have most certainly spiraled down to the point of insanity.

Another thing almost more terrifying struck me. She was everybody else as well, all of humanity. For some, this is what their lives would become if hit by the wrong set of circumstances—addictions and bondages, whether drugs, greed, sexual immorality, or self-obsession. For others, this was a picture of what lurked inside—chaos, anarchy, torment, fear, empty pleasure, self-love, self-hate, insecurity. Whether just inside, or both inside and out, their helpless estate left misery and hopelessness.

I felt Almighty's heart beating inside me. It started beating faster and faster. I finally came close enough that the woman saw me. When our eyes met, she cowered down and became quiet. I stepped toward her carefully and when I came within a few feet of her, she began to back up. "What's your name," I asked? She didn't answer. "What's your name?" I tried again, a little louder. She responded by looking away. "I just heard you crying and wondered what was wrong."

"What do you care?" She retorted.

Her words made me question if I should be here, but since I didn't know the answer, I decided to stay for a little bit. I had seen too many people find refuge in Almighty and she seemed worse off than anyone.

"My name is Simone," she said finally.

"I don't know what's troubling you, but I think I know someone who can help."

"There's no human being that could do anything for me," she said with certainty and sadness.

"You're right about that," I said. "The one I'm speaking of isn't exactly human."

"Then how in the world can this creature understand anything about what it's like to be human?"

"Oh, He's experienced at being human. He took the form of a man and experienced every temptation and trial known to man. He loves us that much, and yet He has power to actually help."

"You're speaking in fairytales," she said, raising her voice and turning away again. She started muttering under her breath and her voice began to elevate while she paced back and forth. Grabbing rocks, she hurled them at the graffiti-covered wall under the bridge.

I turned to walk away.

"Wait, don't go," she whimpered. "I haven't felt this kind of peace in a long time."

I stopped and turned around. Almighty's heart started to beat inside me. He was grieving for her through me. I stared at her. "How can I help you?"

She shook her head. "You can't. I've had my heart broken too many times."

Stepping toward her, I said, "The one who made your heart will never break it."

For the next few minutes, she swung back and forth between bouts of insanity and almost catatonic stillness and silence. I jumped back when she screamed at me in a masculine voice, "Get outta here and take all your tinker bells with you!"

"Alright, I'm going," I said and left.

That night, I tossed and turned. There was something very off about that woman. She was in control and then out of control.

I heard Almighty's voice that night in a vision. "This woman is being held captive by a tormenting spirit. I want you to go and cast it out of her using my name and my authority."

"What? No, absolutely not. You're on your own with this one. It's not my place. I'm not the one to do this. I can't. I don't want to involve myself in that kind of chaos. It's above me, beyond me. There's no way." After I had vehemently refused Almighty's request, I rolled over in bed and tried to go to sleep. I felt like Jonah, refusing to go to Nineveh. My spirit was a storm. My bed became the waves as I tossed in it. I finally fell asleep and was awakened an hour later by Almighty singing.

He was singing songs for Simone. It was disturbing to say the least. "Simone you are my heart's delight. Your voice is sweet and lovely. I long and crave with desperate hands to touch and taste your beauty. I've watched you agonize in life, and I've agonized for you. I spilled my blood, my dreams, my pride for you to love me too. You are chained to fear and misery and I want you to be free, but there's no way for your bonds to break if you won't come to me."

As I listened to Almighty going on and on about this woman He obviously had such a passion for, I grew extraordinarily uncomfortable. It was unbearable to see how much He loved her. I could hardly contain the emotion that was welling up inside of me. "I surrender Almighty," I whispered. "If you love her that much, then I do too." After I said this, I instantly fell asleep.

The next morning, I woke up on a mission to bring Simone to Almighty. I made my way down to the bridge where she was curled up, arms around her knees, rocking back and forth restlessly. She was startled to see me, and I think happy.

"I can't be like this anymore. I'm in prison, help me," she said in desperation.

'Can I pray for you and speak against all that's tormenting you? I don't have any power by myself, but it's Almighty's name and authority that I'm using."

"Did He give you permission for this," she said finally.

"Actually, it was more like a command," I said, smiling.

"Why?"

"He likes you quite a lot." After I said this, Simone looked more shocked than I'd ever seen her. So, I came close to her, put my hands on her head and began to pray. I rebuked the tormenting spirits and commanded them to leave using Almighty's authority. When I opened my eyes, she was smiling and taking deep, unsteady breaths.

"Amazing! I have peace in my body. And in my mind! Everything is fine now."

"Oh, no. I'm taking you with me to Almighty right now," I countered.

"I'm okay. I don't need to go," she said.

"You have to," I insisted. "If you don't find refuge in Almighty, you could be overtaken again—perhaps even worse next time."

Simone looked bewildered and confused. "I can't go. I'm not presentable. I'm dirty."

"He's the only one who can make you clean," I said with certainty.

"But I'll feel ashamed."

"He's the only one who can take away your shame."

"But I don't want to subject Him to my issues. I just want to get it together a little bit, then I will feel better about going before Him."

"Simone, don't you get it? You'll never get it together and have any kind of help for your issues without Him. He doesn't want a fake relationship with you. You don't have to try to clean yourself up. If you could, you would have no need for Him. He wants you to be honest, to come into the light and allow all the things that you want to hide to be exposed, so He can heal you." As I spoke, Simone looked more confused. I became perplexed. "Look, you don't really know Him yet, but you will, and once you know Him, things will become clearer for you."

She fell silent, staring at the ground. "It's just that I have all these drug addictions and I have an addictive personality."

"Well," I said, smiling with excitement, "when you realize how loved you are by Him, you'll get addicted to that." Her eyes grew wide. The whole concept of Almighty being interested in her was foreign. What would she think if she knew how extreme it was? If she had heard Him singing love songs, longingly over her?

After a long silence, she peered into my eyes. "I want to meet Him."

Sighing in relief, I said, "All right, let's go find Him." With that, we were on our way.

Out of all the people I met and talked to about Almighty, the most interesting was a man I met in the park. He was by far the most severe case because He didn't feel He had a need. He had a sense of false peace and a confidence and hope in temporal securities. I guess he had hope in his own capabilities, which seemed to be working out for him. I sat down beside him on a park bench and commented on how I liked his bright green shoes. I told him about my life, how Almighty had saved me, and loved me, and how happy I felt to be loved by Him.

"I guess some people need to have something to believe in to give them peace," he responded.

"Yes, but I'm an intelligent person, and I wouldn't feel comfortable believing in something I didn't know was truth," I said.

"I see your point, and I can see that you completely believe in this being you refer to as Almighty. Since you are an intelligent person, however, I don't understand how you ended up with those kinds of concepts in your head. I don't see the need to worship anybody or anything."

"You do have a need to worship the creator of all things," I responded.

"Then, tell me something," he said, raising his voice. "Why am I not aware of this need that you say I have?"

I paused and pondered the question. "I have a need for food. If I stop eating, I'll stop being hungry and I can go on like that for awhile. In fact, the longer I go without food, the less hungry I'll be. After about forty days, I'll be aware of my hunger, but at that point it will be too late because I'll have started to die. My body will start to eat itself, and I'll die of starvation. I hope you realize you are hungry before you start to die. It's too important of an issue to ignore."

"Maybe I'll consider that when I become aware of my own mortality," he muttered under his breath.

I stood up and smiled. He nodded at me, and I walked away.

A few days later, I was washing dishes and thinking about the man I met in the park. I was so deep in thought, I forgot I was washing knives. I cried out in pain as the blade cut deep into my hand. I grabbed a cloth and wrapped it around my hand tightly to try to contain the bleeding. It was such a deep wound that I had to rush to the emergency room to get stitches. The nurse put a heavy-duty, special bandage on it and had me stay in the waiting room until they could get to me to stitch it up.

As I sat in the corner holding my hand, I noticed another girl sitting in the corner by herself holding her wrist. She also had a bandage wrapped around it. Crying had left her face red and her eyes bloodshot. I was intrigued and even felt pity. She looked so lost and alone, like an abused puppy that may have grown some fangs. My heart began to beat at the familiarly rapid pace. I tried to calm myself down, but it wouldn't stop. And then I realized it was Almighty's heart beating. I moved closer to her, and she cowered farther into her corner. 'What's your name," I asked softly?

She hesitated then said, "Nora."

I smiled, "I'm Eppy."

"Hi Eppy," she whispered and looked away.

"What happened to you," I asked.

She didn't look at me, just kept staring at the wall in the other direction. "I tried to kill myself," she said finally.

"Why?" I blurted, instantly regretting the question. I remembered how I was before Almighty found me. The state of mind I was in was severe. Suicide would not have been too far of a cry for me. Thinking about it now, it sounded utterly stupid. "What I mean is, what drove you to that point?"

She turned back and studied me, as if to determine if she could trust me. "I have nothing. I'm empty, alone, and I have a broken heart."

"I know someone who can heal you," I offered. "He can give you hope and a reason to live."

"Who?"

"Almighty is His name, the Creator of all things. By Him, all things exist, and through Him all creatures have purpose. He is overwhelmingly beautiful and wonderful, gentle and kind. He is filled with love and patience and perfection."

"Good for him," she answered, anger tightening her mouth. "What on god's green earth could I possibly have in common with him?"

It was an interesting question to ponder. I looked at her reddening bandage and the answer occurred to me. "He has scars on His wrist, too."

She stared at me. "Did He try to kill Himself?"

"No, but He willing allowed Himself to be killed."

"He must have been totally depressed. I can understand why He would be, being so perfect, gentle and kind in a world like this."

I smiled, "Actually, He is the happiest person I know."

A weary frown tugged on her lips. "Then why would He willingly let someone to kill Him?"

"He is a hopeless romantic, utterly and totally in love with His creation. He died as a willing sacrifice for sin. Someone had to do it, for without the shedding of blood there is no forgiveness of sin. We would all be doomed to self-made misery. We could never be allowed in the presence of Perfection. Therefore, we would have an absence of joy, pleasure and peace forever. All that would remain would be blackness." I paused, quieting my exuberance. "Do you want to come meet Him?"

"I'm ashamed and embarrassed about my scars."

"You don't have to be. He is the most humble, kind, and merciful person I know. You'll feel completely at rest in His presence. Besides, He still has His scars too."

Nora studied me, glanced down and then looked back. "All right," she said. "If he's so wonderful, I guess I don't have to be timid."

I grinned, excitement dancing in my soul. That very night, I brought her into His presence and her whole life changed. She discovered hope for the first time. She moved from near death to eternal life.

CHAPTER 8

DISCIPLINE

After Nora met Almighty, she was filled with gratitude to me for introducing her, though I didn't really do anything special. She'd been thirsty and I brought her to the fountain. She was in poverty, and I shared the treasure I'd found. It made me feel great to think how I was spreading Almighty's name in the valleys and over the mountains. I was setting the captives free, healing the broken, speaking Almighty's heart! I was chosen, therefore I was special.

I could see that the reason Almighty had placed so much value on me was because I had tremendous value! Watching others, I began to realize I was doing much more than they were for Almighty, at least as far as I could tell. I was gifted, and I was blessed, and my blessings were in part due to my decisions and my good behavior. I delighted in myself, delirious about the untapped potential in me.

Having been absent for a long time, I was mildly surprised when Adversary visited me. Since I was at such a spiritual strong point in my life, I didn't resist him, figuring I could handle Him. He chose to follow me on my walks in the cool of the day. As long as He built me up and didn't tear me down, I tolerated him. And that was exactly what He did. In honesty, I began to enjoy his company.

"I'm really impressed with you," He said one day as we went on our walk. "You are doing such an incredible job of helping people. Do you realize how much you are needed and how rare you are? Look around, there are very few out there like you with such a good heart."

His affirmation surprised me, made me feel great. He was supporting what I was doing to help Almighty. "You're right," I responded. "I finally understand why Almighty is so infatuated with me."

"With all you're doing to help others, you need to spend more time focused on building up yourself," he continued. "Positive thoughts, happy thoughts—whatever it takes for you to feel good. You deserve it. You've earned it."

Some of the things He was saying seemed to contradict some of the things Almighty had said, but it felt good, felt right.

"Your feelings are an important part of you. Never deny them or yourself. In fact, I think it's a grave mistake to deny yourself. Almighty made His entire world and existence all about you. Take the hint. He wants you to continue with that also, to make your world all about you. Don't you get it? You're like a superhero. You have special powers and gifts other people don't have. You are dynamic. It's all for Almighty ultimately, but you need to recognize the greatness in you, give yourself some of the glory on a more regular basis."

I liked what I was hearing, and it seemed somewhat valid, so I allowed Adversary to visit me daily, discussing this matter. It planted within me a new mindset, one in which I was the center of my world. At first, it was a pleasant experience, but then it bored me, eventually becoming utterly sickening and intolerable. Then, because this mindset had now permeated my life, I didn't know how to rid myself of it. Why hadn't I listened to Almighty?

Adversary had been subtle. Why did I entertain all those ridiculous notions? I felt as though I was carrying a hundred and fifty-pound corpse on my back. The weight of self was crushing. It only got worse when I tried by myself and through myself to get rid of myself. My flesh was so weak. I battled myself, striving for freedom, yet dabbling into pride and selfish ambition.

I missed Almighty, but knew I needed to be humble in His presence. It was a natural prerequisite. He made me feel like a child, so carefree, yet I didn't want to see Him right now, embarrassed at my behavior. Almighty had no tolerance for arrogance, but for some reason, He had a pretty high tolerance for me. How that works out, I am not completely sure.

That night I fell asleep quickly and deeply, but I awoke at midnight twisting and turning, thinking about Almighty. I cried softly, but no tears came. My spirit ached with longing, and my heart began to beat faster when I realized Almighty was knocking at my door. I wanted to hide under my bed. The knocking and my heartbeat faded into one sound. I knew He would not stop knocking, and I had too much adrenalin to ignore it. With a trembling hand, I opened the door slowly, and He entered. I made a split-second decision not to humble myself before Him, but to remain obstinate and defiant like a child throwing a temper tantrum. I stood tall, staring into His eyes, unrelenting, attempting to dominate everything.

"SIT.... DOWN," He said, his voice stern, authoritative. I found myself sitting in a chair, not knowing how I got there, peering up at Him. He stood above me and found my eyes. "You know I love you Eppy, and those I love I rebuke and discipline. So be zealous and repent." After He said this, He placed His hand on my cheek and began to stroke it softly. I felt a sting go through my entire body, as though I was running through a raspberry patch, the thorns scraping my skin.

"Make it stop," I screamed.

"No," He answered simply.

I tried to push His hand off my face, but He was stronger, and it didn't budge. My eyes jerked up. His face held a calm serenity, only love in His eyes, no anger. Oddly enough, it was reassuring gazing into His face as He disciplined me. Even though His hand corrected, His eyes comforted. "Please stop, Almighty," I begged.

He didn't stop, but lifted His left hand and touched my other cheek. Thankfully, this touch was not painful, but held me steady until it was over. Finally, He removed both hands, leaving me aching all over. He pulled up a chair next to me and sat with His head in His hands, grieving and disturbed. He obviously didn't enjoy inflicting pain on me.

Even though I felt sore and humiliated, I couldn't stop gazing at Him. Why would He do this to me if He didn't want to? What was the necessity of it? Even though it was not a pleasant experience, I felt relieved of self. Surprisingly, being put back in this place of humility, under His power, brought freedom again.

Without saying a word, He picked me up and put me on His lap. He held me desperately, as if His entire existence depended on it. My mind raced. He had just punished me, and now He was pouring out extreme amounts of affection. I started to cry. I was completely broken. The sting of this experience had overcome me, and I knew it would stay with me for many days to come.

After several hours had passed, Almighty carried me to my bed and covered me with blankets. He kissed me tenderly on my head and told me to go to sleep. He started for the door and then turned around to gaze at me one last time. "I am going to dream about you tonight," He said. "You're always with me." Then He turned and shut the door behind Him.

After Almighty left, I immediately fell asleep. I dreamed that He was taking me by the hand out to the wilderness to a quiet place where I could clearly hear His voice and hear His soft, intimate whispers. The farther away we got from the city, the more the loud noises faded into the background. His voice was all I could hear. I noticed I didn't like the wilderness, preferring distraction, but He was calling me away. "Come away, come away with me."

When I awoke, I was confronted by the pain that had been inflicted on me the night before. I also awoke feeling peace and a sense of rightness. Somehow, Almighty's discipline had resulted in these things. Each day, the work He'd done continued to magnify in my life. Although the sting of His hand had not yet subsided, I began to have even more joy and rest. He'd been protecting me from myself.

Convinced of His good for me, I submitted to His authority and cast down resistance and opposition, even though I had not yet been released from the pain. I remembered Almighty's words, His kindness, His mystery and heart—most of all His exceeding affection toward me. My awareness of these realities kept me from anger and bitterness.

A few weeks passed, and He came to me again in the night. I heard Him knocking on my door and my heart began to beat again, matching the rhythm of the knock. I ran to the door and opened it. There was something in His hand. Before I had a chance to peek, He lifted me and carried me to my couch.

"I have torn you to pieces, but I will heal you. I have greatly wounded you, but I will bind you up." He held out a jar. "This is healing balm. Just lay back and let me soothe your injuries." He pulled out some of a thick substance and rubbed it gently over my face. The pain instantly began to subside. My whole body felt as though warm oil had been poured over it. Then He dabbed some on my feet and began to massage in the balm. The pain was not only relieved, but I felt pleasure in my spirit to a degree unknown until that moment. I started to think the pain was worth this healing pleasure. When He finished, He lingered, gazing at me, drinking me in with His eyes.

"I want to tell you a story," He said, leaning His face close to mine. "There was once a Shepherd who had many little sheep that He loved very much. Whenever wild animals came to try to devour the lambs, the Shepherd always protected them, even putting Himself at risk. One day, one of His little lambs decided to run away. The Shepherd loved this lamb very much. If He didn't do something, His lamb would be in danger of being eaten by one of the wild animals, or at least be lost and confused, alone in the wilderness.

"So, the shepherd left the other sheep, found the lamb and brought him back. However, the lamb kept running away. One day the Shepherd chased the lamb again and found him caught in the bushes. A coyote was nearby, ready to kill him. The Shepherd rescued him just in time. He then led the lamb down to the river and there took this staff and broke the lamb's leg. Since the lamb couldn't walk now, the shepherd carried him on His shoulders until his leg recovered.

"The lamb spent a lot of time in the Shepherd's arms while his leg was healing. In that time, he bonded with the Shepherd. By the time the leg healed, the lamb never again wandered away, but stayed by the Shepherd's side. So, you see, sometimes love involves pain and discipline, yet it always involves healing and results in peace and righteousness." Almighty's story was so simple a child could understand it and a theologian could miss it.

It was days after He left when I experienced full recovery. The discipline Almighty had given to me slowed me down and drew me back to His side. When I thought about Almighty's nature and character, it became obvious that everything He did had purpose, and usually a very specific, intricately thought-out purpose. I questioned to what degree I believed this.

I felt restored back to Almighty's side after my recent prideful wonderings, though in reality He had never left me. I smiled. A spirit of rest had descended, leaving me content just to be by His side, understanding that was what He wanted all along. We took long walks in the cool of the day. It was the best time of my life. I abandoned all thoughts of personal ambition and gain. I separated myself from distraction and obsession. I simply went on walks with Him every day. I loved to talk, and He loved to listen, yet I found that the more listening I did, the happier I was. When He spoke, I felt liberation and excitement, hopeful and encouraged. Many things He taught changed my thinking. Faith pumped through my veins like blood. Nothing I did or thought or felt mattered to me. All joy was contained in Him and being with Him.

CHAPTER 9

HIDING IN ALMIGHTY

One day, Adversary showed up at my door. He was on a mission to kill, steal and destroy. It wasn't long before he turned my entire world upside down. People closest to me died. I was abandoned by family members. Everything I owned was destroyed. I lost my livelihood. He had lowered me to a heap of rubble.

If that wasn't enough, he towered over me, taunting and confusing me. He said Almighty was responsible for these disasters and losses. Then he brought accusations against me, saying I was responsible. It was my sin and my failures that were the cause of all this horror.

"Leave me alone," I cried.

"Not on your life," he said, circling me. "You are such a fool, such a prideful little twit. You are insignificant and valueless. Do you think Almighty really, truly cares about you? Why would all this disaster and death be happening to you if Almighty was truly involved in your life?"

Adversary enjoyed tormenting me this way. It was nothing new, but regardless, it still caused me to question. It hurt when I allowed it any room in my mind. Even though Adversary had destroyed my entire life, there was one thing he couldn't take from me—my relationship with Almighty. He could try to damage it, but it would always be intact. Almighty had promised that it was His grip on me that was my salvation.

In thinking about it, my relationship with Almighty was the most important thing anyway. I could have my closest friend die, be abandoned by my family, lose my livelihood and be sitting in a whirlwind of confusion and complaints, but if I had Almighty, I had everything. Comparatively, none of that other stuff even mattered.

On the other hand, if I didn't have Almighty, I had nothing. He truly was my core. In fact, I wouldn't have even known how much He was my core if I hadn't experienced everything taken away. He was my greatest need, my only need.

My eyes swept the room. Everything in my house lay destroyed and broken. Adversary began to dance around me, chanting repetitiously about my worthlessness. Then out of the corner of my eye, I saw an object hurling toward me. Adversary had grabbed a kitchen knife and flung it with great accuracy in my direction. I darted out of the way, the blade barely missed my head.

I realized in that moment Adversary was out to destroy more than my world, he was after my life. He began to find other sharp objects to throw at me. Most of the time he missed, but sometimes he would wound me. My body suffered cuts and bruises as the battle intensified. I grabbed whatever I could find for a shield, but nothing proved impenetrable.

Bleeding, I realized I couldn't fight this battle on my own. Adversary was strong, his words sharp, his lies devastating. His weapons were piercing. I tried to hide behind things, but nothing covered me. I raced from him, but he followed me relentlessly. His tactics were shrewd, the battle severe. I knew I had to find Almighty, so I darted out the door and ran farther and farther, the rain pouring down, washing my cuts.

In a frantic state, and with Adversary trailing close behind me, I searched everywhere for Almighty. "Almighty, where are you?" I whispered, my voice hoarse. I remembered the day I ran away from Him, the night I darted out into the darkness away from His love. His mysterious passion for me had been hard to receive. It delighted my soul but being exposed in the light had made me uncomfortable.

Now I was running toward Him with all my soul. I needed Him desperately, needed His protection, but where was He? Miraculously, I continued to dodge Adversary's many weapons of choice. I fled into the dark woods and felt like I was losing him. Having turned many corners in an effort to escape, I didn't recognize the path. Thick, heavy fog hung in the night, obscuring the ground before me.

I heard running close behind me, getting closer and closer, the sound terrifying. Soon I would be overtaken and at the mercy of Adversary. The footsteps were now only a few feet behind me. All of a sudden, arms lifted me and carried me through the forest. I turned my head to look at my captor. It was Almighty!

He carried me violently through the woods, running with purposeful intensity. I held on for dear life, the thick fog veiling His face and cloaking our path. Suddenly, I realized Adversary was still pursuing me. I heard him on the trail again, rapidly gaining ground. I wondered why Almighty was running. He could take Adversary out with one look of His eyes.

"Where are we going?" I whimpered.

"I'm bringing you to a secret place," He panted.

He came to a sudden stop. I could just make out the edge of a cave cut in the side of a cliff. Holding me tightly, He rushed me inside where it was cold and damp. Bats hung from the roof of the cave. I didn't like the bats, not at all. I shrieked and clung onto Almighty's arm. He grinned at me and my petty fears.

Then he did something I wouldn't have imagined was possible unless I had seen and experienced it for myself. He pulled me back to the deepest, dampest corner of the cave and set me down in the dirt. A chill crept down my spine as bats fluttered around the cave. He curled my body into a ball and wrapped His body around me. Huge majestic, birdlike wings sprung out of His back. Each wing was the entire span of His body. He wrapped His wings around me and covered me. I didn't even know He had wings. My body became warm as from a heater. The "secret place" where He hid me was underneath the shelter of His wings.

I heard Adversary approaching. He was on a conquest for my total destruction. He passed by the cave flinging arrows and knives into the darkness before him. Though he couldn't see or hear us, a loose arrow flew into the cave and pierced one of Almighty's wings. He cringed from the piercing pain, but He didn't cry out. Blood drenched the pure white feathers. Except for Almighty's shallow, ragged breathing, we remained still and quiet for thirty minutes until certain that Adversary would not return.

Almighty let go long enough to remove the arrow, pushing it through the rest of the wing until it's point appeared, then the shaft. With a mighty effort, He grasped it and drew it out. Wrapping his wing with healing leaves from nearby, He bandaged it up.

As we listened, an army of impish demons approached, yelling out blasphemies. He held me in His arms while covering me with His wings as the hunters flew past the cave. I shivered. The battle was still very much alive and active.

"The demons are hunters on a heavily commissioned pursuit," Almighty whispered.

I felt safe under His wings, but I began to feel restless and started to squirm. Almighty held me still so we wouldn't attract attention, but I also couldn't move. This made me even more restless. I wanted to leave this dark, oppressive cave. I longed for home and fought to escape this ordeal, but He overpowered me and held me down forcefully. I kept fighting.

"Be still!" he yelled, rebuking me. He was above me, pinning me down. I fought back, then realized I was fighting against Almighty, the one trying to protect me. With His hand still covering my mouth to make me shut up, He leaned close and began whispering gently in my ear, "Eppy, be still, be silent, be still."

I mumbled and he lifted His hand. "I need to do something, I need to get away," I argued.

"No, you need to be still," he answered back gently. After I agreed to stop yelling, He removed His hand from my mouth. He pulled me onto His lap and wrapped His arms around me, still covering me with His wings.

I glanced down at the hands holding me and noticed something on His palms. I moved His hand to look closer. It was my name, EPPY, in capital letters, but it wasn't written, it was carved. Almighty had carved my name into His hand with a knife. It was scabbed over and beginning to scar. I looked up into warm eyes beaming down at me.

Questions flew through my mind. Why would He carve my name into the palm of His hand? It was not as if He just scraped the surface of His skin. He made deep gouges in His hands. I wondered when He did this. I laid my head against His chest and thought about His hands, those hands that pulled me from sin and darkness. His hands, filled with so much power, had caused me so much comfort, so much pleasure, yet so much pain. With His hands, He wounded me, and He healed me. Now, He had carved my name in His palms.

As I sat on His lap, He began stroking my cheek with His fingers, reading my thoughts. Then I remembered something I'd almost forgotten, something that happened long ago. I remembered how His hands willingly took the spikes for my sin. By Himself, with His own hands, He redeemed me. Though He was the shepherd, and I was His little lamb, He became a lamb and was led willingly to the slaughter.

These were the same hands that had knocked on my door night after night, day after day for years. I had rarely opened the door to let our relationship gain any momentum. He had carried it, and He carried me. Two little tears ran down my cheeks when I thought about His obsession with me. He wiped them away with His thumb.

"Come on Eppy," He said, pulling me up by the hand. "We can go back now."

It was a long journey back. Almighty took paths that were safe, but they were harder to travel. We walked for several hours, and I became exhausted. "I'm tired Almighty," I whined.

Without a word, He picked me up and carried me the rest of the way home.

The next few days, I found myself daydreaming about Almighty taking me into the cave and hiding me under His wings. I thought about how His hands had my name carved into them. I became obsessed with them and what they were capable of—like spinning the world into being.

CHAPTER 10

I'M YOUR DAD

One night I heard Almighty knocking at my door. This was not out of the ordinary, but I usually ignored it. Having slipped back into my old habits, I would let the noise fade into the sound of the clock as I fall asleep. Sometimes, even though I heard the knocking, I convinced myself that He was not really there.

Tonight, however, I had a deep longing for Him. When I heard Him, I rushed out of bed and ran toward the door. I was filled with anticipation and desire and knew He was drawing me to Himself. I opened the door and found Him standing there with grapes in one arm and bread in the other.

"May I come in and dine with you?" He asked.

I looked into His eyes, eyes filled with such depth and wisdom, as though they carried the hopes of the whole world. I moved out of the way, and He entered.

We sat down and I watched as He ripped the bread apart and took the grapes in His hand, squeezing the juice into a cup. It was a poetic movement, artistic and significant, every little look and touch held meaning. He handed me a piece of the bread and told me to eat it. "It is my body broken for you." He then handed me the juice and told me to drink it. "It's my blood poured out for you. Do this to remember me."

This act reminded me of how He had been torn, and how He bled to take the punishment for my sins. It was a beautiful thought. It reminded me of how loved I was, of how far He went to redeem me. There was so much comfort and pleasure being in His presence that I never wanted to leave. We shared the bread and juice, the communion sweet. I felt a sense of sadness for all the days I had let go by without communing with Him. Yet, my regret was followed by joy all wrapped up in this one moment. He expressed to me how much He enjoyed my company and how this night had been such a pleasure to Him. And then He was quiet. He looked down as if dissatisfied.

"What's wrong?" I asked.

"You don't know me the way I want you to know me," He said, delving into my eyes.

That seemed odd. I thought I knew Him better than I ever had in my life. He was Almighty, powerful, ever loving, self-willed, self-sacrificing, all righteous and all knowing. Curious, I asked, "What do you mean?"

"Why do you call me Almighty?"

"Because it's your name, it's the essence of who you are."

"But who am I to you?"

Once again Almighty had lost me. I didn't know what He was talking about. So, I let Him do all the talking.

"I am your dad," He said, looking at me as though I should know this by now. But I didn't know it, and it shocked me. It seemed beyond ridiculous. He is good, I am bad. He is strong, I am weak. I am selfish and He is the epitome of selflessness. He is immortal and the list went on and on.

It seemed that usually when you were someone's child, you looked like him, acted like and thought like him. There were many similarities. Yet, between me and Almighty, I just didn't see it. I thought back to my earthly father and wondered, If Almighty had raised me, would have turned out differently? Deep down, I longed to be like Him, and I wished I were related to Him. "How can this be?" I asked.

"I adopted you," He said. "You are my child, and you are now royalty. You will share in my inheritance. All the privileges bestowed on natural born children I give to you." He smiled. "Do you think you could get used to thinking of me as your dad?"

I was surprised about this, but I wasn't totally shocked. I was starting to get used to Almighty throwing curve balls at me. It was just His usual unusualness. But really, my dad and royalty? Why in the world did He choose me? "I can get used to it," I answered slowly. "But are you sure you really want to adopt me?"

"I already have," He said. "It's done."

"When did this happen?"

"I knew you before you were conceived. When you received my redemption and came under my covenant, you became my child. I bought you with my own blood. You are mine."

"So, what does this mean? I don't completely understand."

"Let me explain it to you in detail," He said. "My being your dad means you don't have to watch your own back anymore. I am your protector. I will take vengeance on anyone who tries to hurt you. I am your refuge and shelter—a very present help in times of trouble.

"I will correct you if you go astray only because I love you and want the best for you. No weapon formed against you will prosper, and every tongue that rises against you I will condemn. This is your heritage because your righteousness is from me. I will provide all your needs according to my riches in glory. As earthly parents who are evil know how to give good gifts to their children, how much more will I, being all loving and merciful, give good and perfect gifts to you?

"I want you to ask, to cry out to me, to trust me even in times of trouble and affliction. I want you to trust my love, and to know that I am working all things together for the good because you've received my love and are called according to my purpose. Even if you're killed for trusting me, you can die smiling because you know you'll be instantly transported into my presence.

"No one can condemn you, for I have justified you, no one can accuse you, for I have died in your place and have risen for you. If I am for you, who's going to be against you? I am seated at the right hand of God and am praying for you. Nothing can separate you from my love."

My mind raced at His words.

He continued, "And one more thing, I'd like it very much if you would call me Daddy."

"Uh, okay...Daddy," I responded, not knowing what else to say. I wanted so desperately to believe what He was telling me—that I could trust all these extravagant promises He was making. It became clear that believing Him came down to a simple choice. I could accept His words and receive the benefit of believing, or not.

But why did He want me to call Him Daddy? What was that about? It was almost as if He saw me as a little child, unable to make right decisions and protect myself. Or He saw me as easily led around, controlled and confused. Yet, He wanted to be my father and take care of me. To me, the name "Daddy" seemed a little over the top, but I knew He was the essence of passion. In fact, compared to Him, I felt apathetic, dull. I decided to let His words sink in as much as possible. His words were cleansing.

I would try to think of Him as my Father. I communed with my own soul about it and after meditating heavily on that reality and after a few days, found myself in a euphoric state. Unfortunately, it was too hard of a concept for me to grasp, so I went back to calling him Almighty. I was far more comfortable with it.

One night, I lay awake thinking of my birthday the following day. Sleep evaded me until, around midnight, I got out of bed and went outside to breathe the fresh air. Almighty stood on my doorstep looking at the night sky. "I want to bring you to a special place. Let's go," He said softly, taking my hand and beginning to lead me.

"Right now? It's the middle of the night. Come back in the morning,"

"I don't want you to miss out on what I want to show you," He said. "You can't sleep anyway. Where's your sense of adventure?"

"What about sleep, Almighty, isn't that important to You?"

"I love sleep," He said, "but I love you more. I promise you'll feel more rested in the morning having spent these next few hours with me."

"Ok." I said finally, letting Him pull me along on our next excursion. I was curious to discover where He was taking me, certain it would be interesting. Having known Almighty for a while, my curiosity increased, anxious to see what was around the corner and over the horizon. Although I resisted, it had become like an addiction.

We walked and talked for a couple of hours. In the darkness, I couldn't see where He was taking me. In fact, it was so dark that I couldn't even see what was around me. So, I held onto Almighty's hand and let Him have control of where we were going and how we were getting there. All at once, I smelled the ocean and eventually began to hear the sound of waves.

We arrived on a sandy beach. The moon appeared suddenly and lit up the whole area, reflecting little pools of light on the water. It was beautiful! As we got closer to the water, I saw words written on the sand, *Happy Birthday Eppy. Love, your Maker.*

He looked at me and smiled when He saw me reading it.

I hadn't told Him it was my birthday. The corners of my mouth curled up as I caught the delight in his face—I couldn't help it.

"Let's go for a swim," He said suddenly and began to run toward the ocean.

"Wait, that water is freezing! It won't be any fun."

"Oh, come on. Don't you trust me?" He said, turning around with a playful smirk.

"Yes, I trust you, but the water is like ice, that's an objective fact."

"I have powers that you don't know about," He said, still smiling. "Or at least you've forgotten about."

"What are you going to do, make the water warm? I didn't know you were in the habit of going against the laws of nature."

At this point, Almighty began walking toward me with a dominating stare. I felt intimidated but couldn't move. When He reached me, He wrapped His arms around me and held me close without a word. I felt the warmth of His body rush through mine. He held my head in His hands and placed His mouth near my ear and whispered, "Eppy, why do you have such a need to be in control? I wish you would just let go. Let go of your inhibitions. Let go of your fears, and just have a reckless trust in me. You would experience much more freedom." With that, He took my hand and led me to the water. He stepped in first without flinching.

I followed. It was freezing. It felt like thousands of needles pricking my skin, like liquid ice. And it wasn't just cold and uncomfortable, it was painful. The deeper I submerged myself, the more painful it became. I watched Almighty swimming contently, floating on His back, gazing at the stars above Him. I was very aware of the icy water numbing my skin. "I'm getting out!" I declared and began to move toward the shore.

"No, no, just a little longer," Almighty protested. "Trust me."

"Alright, fine," I pouted. I figured if I went numb, I wouldn't be able to feel anything anyway. Then an amazing thing happened. Right when I was at the point where I felt like I couldn't take it anymore, something changed. I felt a rush go through my entire body. My skin began to tingle. I had a sensation of ecstasy shooting through me from my toes all the way up to my head. It wasn't even that the water became warm. It was still freezing, but my body changed. I was now experiencing pleasure instead of pain. I wanted to go deeper in the water. I wanted to be near Almighty. I swam out to Him.

"Do you know I named all of these stars," He said, continuing to gaze at the sky.

I floated next to Him. "Tell me their names."

"Well, that one is "Rigil Kentaurus," and that one is "Canis Majoris," and that one is called 'My Bride.' It's my favorite."

"Why is it your favorite?"

"Because I named it after you," He said, looking at me, His laughing eyes now serious.

I explored His eyes, not understanding the connection between a star called, My Bride, and me. I let it go but kept looking at Almighty. He had a glow about Him. The kind of glow you have when you're in love. He was so confident, as though His spirit was saying, "I have all the answers." And He did. He was gentle and powerful, intelligent and beautiful. He was all together separate from anyone or anything I had ever known. Just being in His presence brought about intensity and ecstasy.

"You are such a dreamer," I said suddenly.

Almighty drew close to me and stroked my wet cheek. "I am a dreamer," He said. "I dream about eternity with you, and I'll keep dreaming."

"Where's your practical side?" I argued, still losing control of my words.

He smiled down at me, holding my face with both hands. "My practical side is when I died for you. Without death, there is no dream."

I felt a hot tear slide down my cheek. My heart beat faster. I wanted to worship Him.

"Come on. Let's go lay in the sand," He said impulsively.

"No, the water feels so good, and it's going to be cold out there."

Almighty laughed. "Eppy you're so predictable—at least your resistance is." He picked me up, threw me over His shoulder and carried me out of the water—with me squirming, of course. Then He laid me in the sand across from where he had written Happy Birthday to me. He lay down beside me and took my hand in His, holding it tightly.

I turned and faced away from Him. The moonlight left a glow around us. I glanced down at my hand, startled at the streaks of blood smudged on it. I turned around and stared at Almighty's hand. He had freshly carved my name into his hand with a knife, only it was on the outside of his hand this time. It was as if He were advertising His affections for me to the world. The wounds were still raw, but they were beginning to heal. I looked into His eyes. I almost heard them speaking to me, "I love you so much Eppy, more than you'll ever know."

CHAPTER 11

FACING FEARS

We watched the sun come up together. Almighty would watch the sun come up with me every single morning if I were up for it. Morning was such a happy time. Even the dawn seemed to whisper, I love you. As the morning drifted on, I became restless and decided it was time to go.

Sensing my departure, Almighty moved His face toward me and put His hand on my arm. "Meet me outside your door tomorrow morning," He said. "I want to do something, or rather I want you to do something that is going to bring you into extreme freedom. But it's going to be intense."

Intense? I didn't like the sound of that at all. Half of what Almighty said to me was too nerve-racking to face, and the other half seemed ridiculously too good to be true. "Almighty, why do we have to do something intense? Let's just do the same thing we did today. I'm okay with going in the water now."

He stepped toward me to embrace me before I left. These days He had a plastered smile on His face almost constantly. It was because of me. He loved me. "Just trust me, My Eppy, it's going to be okay."

So, I left. I thought about how He called me My Eppy. I had never heard Him refer to me that way before. It was a possessive term. He was certainly possessively jealous over me. That I knew, and that I had come to accept. If I put one little, tiny thing before Him, it proved to be detrimental to our relationship. The bazaar thing is that it had more of a negative effect on me when I put something before Him. So, His possessive jealousy was actually more for my own good and my own protection.

I wondered what He had up his sleeve for tomorrow. Well, I would soon find out. I drifted off to sleep thinking about lying in the sand with Almighty, Him stroking my cheek with His hand and telling me He loved me with His eyes, taking a nap on the little birthday love note that He wrote for me in the sand.

The next morning, I was awakened by Him knocking on my door. It felt so early, but I knew His persistent nature, and I promised to meet Him, so I got up. There was a sweet exhilaration in His face. I took His hand, and we were off. Since it was light out, I saw where we were going. It was an off-road, very narrow path. Obviously, very few people had traveled this way before. In fact, the farther along we got, the more nervous I became. "Almighty, are you sure about this?" I asked, looking up at Him.

He just chuckled under His breath and continued leading me forward. Finally, we came to the end of our track. We couldn't go any further because, well, we were at the edge of a cliff. Below the waves were crashing up against the side of the cliff with great force.

"Almighty, let's go back now," I said backing away from the edge.

He didn't budge. He just looked at me. "I want you to jump off this cliff into the water," He said resolutely.

"What? There is absolutely no way you are getting me to jump off this cliff!"

"I want you to be free, but you have fears and insecurities holding you back from total freedom."

I peered into the water, and I felt something in the air. He had taken me to the edge of my greatest fears—fear of not having what I truly, deeply wanted. Fear of experiencing the pain that terrified me. And he wanted me to let go! "Almighty, this is going to traumatize me."

He put out his hand for me to hold. "Do you trust me?" He asked.

I blatantly refused to grab hold of His hand. I took a few steps backward. I felt my body getting hot. Sweat began to bead up on the back of my neck. I wanted to curl up into a ball and cry, but instead, I ran. I turned away from Almighty and darted backward onto the rough, narrow path. Going backward on this narrow path didn't seem natural.

Adversary was standing at the end of the path. I ran toward him. It was the only direction I could go. As I approached him, he opened up his arms to embrace me. I hesitantly allowed this because of the way I was feeling. As his arms closed around me, I felt wrapped in shame. The fear had not left but seemed to follow me. I didn't release it, so it intensified. I wanted to run back to Almighty, but fear and shame held me captive. I was a prisoner.

"It's okay," Adversary said comfortingly. "You stay right here with me where it's safe. You don't want to go back to Almighty right now. He's very disappointed in you. You need to stay away from Him for a while, give Him some time to cool off. He has a very short fuse."

"Really? That doesn't seem like him. In fact, He always seems pretty above and beyond when it comes to mercy."

"Yeah, but look how much He's done for you, proving His love time and time again. In return, He asked you to do one little thing and you can't do it. I guarantee it's wearing on Him. One of these days, He's going to snap. It's all building up. You need to prove yourself by your actions. I guarantee it will improve your relationship with Him, and you'll finally feel accepted. You need to give Him a reason to be proud of you."

I tried to think about Adversary's words, but I was so saturated with shame I couldn't even think clearly.

I camped out there for the evening under the stars. Adversary had left, but I sensed him hovering nearby. I looked up at the stars and thought about Almighty and how He had given every single one of them their own unique name. He even named one of them after me, a star called, My Bride, whatever that meant. He was so majestic, so amazing, so perfect. I fell asleep and had visions of Him pursuing me like a hunter in the woods.

I was stranded there for several days. I couldn't move forward, and I couldn't move backwards. Every night, I camped out under the stars, and I heard Almighty speaking to me through them. The message He was giving me was extreme and powerful, but I didn't fully understand it. I just felt it, believed it, and was certain it was something extraordinary. In those moments, I felt temporarily relieved of shame. When I fell asleep, I always heard Almighty running through the forest, chasing me down.

One morning, I woke up and He was sleeping next to me. He obviously had come to me in the night and fallen asleep. When I saw Him, I gasped. I couldn't face Him. I was such a coward. When faced with my fears, I ran away. I was a total, perpetual failure. I quietly stood up and tried to sneak away, but before I could get away, He opened His eyes and looked straight at me. His stare paralyzed me.

"My Eppy," He said.

I was surprised that he would speak to me in such an endearingly possessive way in light of my recent cowardly actions.

"Almighty, I just want to be alone right now."

He held out His hand. "Come to me," He said.

I reluctantly put my hand in His and let Him pull me beside Him. He put His arm around me, and with His other hand, pulled my head onto His chest.

I started to cry. "I'm such a failure and a disappointment, and I'm such a coward. And I'm cursed I know I am. I must be. I'm not making any progress. I am destined to go in circles forever. I am not capable of change."

"Eppy," Almighty said, gently wiping the tears from my face. "You are not cursed because I became a curse for you by hanging on the tree. You are not capable in yourself, but I chose you and I will finish the work that I started in you. I know to yourself, you are a disappointment, a failure and coward, but to me, you are my greatest treasure."

"Almighty, I don't understand you. Everything you say is always good news. How is that even possible? Everything you say defies hopelessness. How can you be so compassionate? I would have destroyed me a long time ago."

Almighty looked into the distance still stroking the tears from my cheek. "I allowed myself to be destroyed for you. Why would I destroy you, the very one I died to save?"

Everything Almighty said was so significant, that I almost had to see into another realm to understand. He continued to comfort me with His hands, His voice and His merciful words. I didn't get it. I fail and He comforts me instead of punishing me. It's as if He has a thing for not giving me the consequences that I deserve, and then turning around giving me all these gifts and all this love that I absolutely, most certainly do not deserve. So, I laid my head on His chest and let Him talk me into accepting myself as He accepts me.

As I sat there, overcome by His love and reminded of His nature, it almost caused me to want to face my fears. In this moment of intimacy with Almighty, I almost felt that I could let Him take me to the edge of the cliff and possibly dare to jump. His everlasting love and His meek and lowly heart were bringing rest to my soul and incinerating my fears. He was worthy of all my trust, all my adoration and my eternal devotion. He had restored my soul.

That night we slept under the stars. I went to sleep with joy in my soul, and I was comforted by Almighty's presence. But I awoke in the middle of the night while Almighty was sleeping and snuck away. I didn't do this because I wanted to get away from Him, but rather, I felt unsettled.

As I walked down the moonlit path in the dark, Adversary's words came into my mind. "You need to prove yourself, and then you'll finally feel accepted. You need to give him a reason to be proud of you." So, I decided to go on a quest. It was completely my idea. Almighty knew nothing about it, and that's what I wanted. I wanted to prove myself once and for all.

At daybreak, I came to the bottom of a mountain that I wanted to climb. I started my journey immediately, pulling myself up the steep, rocky mountain cliff. One handhold and foothold at a time, I climbed for hours. Sweat began to pour down my face. It glistened on my skin. I climbed all day and into the night. Since it was now dark, I couldn't see where I was climbing. I barely found handholds and footholds. Stress filled me with anxiety. I began to cut my hands on the rocks while trying to find holds. They were just small nicks at first, and then they bled profusely. I didn't know how I made it through the night. The next day, I found a wide enough plateau on the rock to rest my body and go to sleep.

I slept for hours out of sheer exhaustion, then awoke as the sun began to go down. I arose and braced myself for the harsh, cold night of climbing ahead. My stomach tightened at the thought of it. As I climbed the mountain, the rocky edges, obscured by the night, scraped my skin. I wiped my sweaty forehead and blood smeared across my face. I climbed for hours, and then I began to cry, sobbing out of anger, stress, and frustration, but I refused to call out to Almighty. I was doing this for Him and would not ask Him for help.

The same cycle continued day in and day out until I finally reached the top. There was a plateau at the top of the mountain with a tree in the middle. I crawled over to the tree, barely having the energy to move. I was a conglomerate of blood, sweat and tears. I curled up in a ball under the tree and fell asleep. I awoke to an icy drizzle stinging my skin.

I sat under the tree contemplating my accomplishment and felt a sense of disappointment. Maybe I didn't climb high enough or sweat and bleed enough. I wondered what Almighty would think of my endeavors. As I sat and stared out into the cold gray sky, something dawned on me. I didn't have a plan for getting down. Did I think I was going to grow wings and fly off the mountain? I looked over the edge of the cliff. It was a long way down. It had taken me days to get to the top. There was no way I could get to the bottom. Climbing down was not an option. The whole mountain was now iced over. There was nothing to grab.

There was only one thing I could do, call out to Almighty for help. This was going to be completely embarrassing. This was something I wanted to do on my own without Him, a kind of offering of effort and self-will, and now I was stuck. I couldn't even move without Him. It had almost entirely backfired. It was utterly humiliating. So, I opened my mouth and called out to Him, first in a sheepish whimper and then in a loud whisper.

I began to cry because the icy rain was hurting my ears and making my fingers and toes feel numb. However, I was mostly crying because I felt so emotionally distraught over this ridiculous predicament I was in. I kept whispering His name, hoping that He would come and hoping that He wouldn't come at the same time.

Then I saw Him. He was standing with His back to me looking over the side of the cliff. He had never stood with his back to me before. It was strange. "Eppy," He said with His back still turned. "Why did you go on this journey?"

"I wanted to prove something to you. I wanted to be the best I could be for you."

"Eppy," He said turning around. "Observe the proud one, his soul is not right within him, but the righteous will live by faith. Do you know what that means?"

I knew my answer would probably be different from His, so I remained silent.

"You don't live by your own blood, sweat and tears," He continued. "You live by my blood, sweat and tears. If you asked me if you should go on this journey, I would have said yes. However, I would've gone with you. You can't just leave me behind, and you don't do things for me. I do things through you. It looks a lot different."

"Different how, what do you mean it looks different?"

"Well, the whole journey would be different. For one thing, I would've been climbing, and you would be on my back. I would've been sweating, bleeding, and crying, and you would've been holding onto me, squeezing me, letting me feel your love. I would've brought you to the top through my effort, but I still would've given you a crown. The only crowns that are given are those that are not earned. You are saved by my gift, through your faith, not by your own effort lest you boast."

Almighty kept reiterating to me what I already knew, but always seemed to forget. One phrase that He said kept coming into my mind, "The righteous will live by faith." How can one live by faith? Is it like food or medicine? I was about to verbalize these very thoughts when Almighty answered me without my even asking.

"Faith is having hope in what you do not see. This kind of hope is the absolute expectation that everything will work out for the good. Hope will not disappoint, that is, if your hope is in me. When you live by faith, you're choosing to live in a state of hope. Hope in what you do not see but know within the very depth of your being exists. You live by this hope. You feed on it. It's what keeps you going."

Observing I was freezing, Almighty wrapped His coat around me and pulled me into His arms.

"Almighty, it seems like no matter what I do, you always make everything okay."

He studied my eyes with a grin. "That's what I do. I make everything okay. The farther away you get from me, the less okay things will be, but the closer you stay, the better, because I will be with you through it all." He grew silent, and I wondered what He was thinking.

"Is something wrong?" I asked.

"No not at all."

"Well, what are you thinking?" I pressed.

"I was wondering when you might apply that truth—my making everything okay—to you facing your fears."

"Oh," I said, lacking a better response.

"Let's reason about this," He continued. "Why don't you trust me in this area? Don't you know that if I ask you to do something, even if you're afraid, it will turn out okay?"

I really couldn't argue with Him. He had a flawless record for faithfulness, kindness and perfection. I've had my share of pain that led to fear, but it was all brought on by me or by an outside source very different from Almighty. In fact, upon reflection, my fear was irrational. Why was it so hard for me to jump, to take risks? It seemed easy to Almighty. In fact, it seemed His favorite thing—a pass-time, a hobby.

"Almighty, why is this so important?" I asked finally.

Searching my face, His usual grin faded. I heard sadness in His voice when He said, "Oh, Eppy, I wish you understood how free I want you to be. There are certain things you can't get beyond right now. You don't see them because you've lived your whole life inside these perimeters. I want to show you what's beyond them, what's beyond the familiar, what's beyond yourself."

I shifted, suddenly uncomfortable. "If I don't see it, then why does it matter?"

"You don't feel a thirty-pound load on your back if you've carried it your whole life. You're used to it. In fact, the thought of removing it would be hard because it feels like a part of you. On the other hand, you don't realize how much lighter you could be, how much freer you could feel, unless you're willing to remove it."

"I just don't want to step into what's uncomfortable for me." I cringed at the whine in my voice.

He just laughed, accepting me no matter what I decided to do. Yet I sensed His longing for what would be best for me. I really didn't need an explanation of why it was so important or what His reasons were. In all reality, I think I just wanted to argue with Him and be obstinate. I knew there was a legitimate reason for anything He would ask me to do, no matter how absurd it seemed to me.

I sighed, a battle raging on the inside. Even knowing what to do, I didn't always want to do it. I fought against myself, justified myself.

The good I wanted to do, I didn't do, and the evil I didn't want to do, I ended up doing. I truly didn't understand how facing my fears and putting myself outside my comfort zone would make me freer. However, I did know that if Almighty said it, it had to be true. I believed Him, yet I was still having trouble bringing myself back to the edge of the cliff.

"Eppy," He whispered. "I was terrified once, so much that my sweat turned into blood."

"What? You were afraid? I didn't even think fear was something you even remotely understood."

He shook His head, face somber, "I have experienced every kind of trial, temptation, and fear known to man, except I've experienced it at a far more intense degree than you could ever know. The anticipation of the cross incited brutal fears within me. I was internally tormented before I was physically tortured."

The thought of Almighty afraid made me uneasy. I knew He experienced temptations and trials, but fear? That defied the very essence of who He is. Why would He allow Himself to go through that? I mean, really, why when He could've stopped it?

Usually when I get to know someone, spend time with them, I grow to understand them, but not Almighty. The longer I knew Him, the more mysterious He became. It was as though He lived His existence in opposition to basic human nature. He had peace in chaos, patience in extreme suffering, mercy and kindness toward those who showed Him extreme brutality and cruelty. Instead of taking rightful vengeance on His enemies, He washed them in His own blood so that they could then become His friends.

I could not for the life of me figure out what made Him tick, except for one thing—me! At every turn, He pursued me, invested in me, taught me, loved me. I was what He dreamed about. The strange thing was, as much as He desired me, He didn't need me. He didn't have any weird dependence on me. He was totally complete by Himself. In fact, I was the needy one, dependent on Him. This reality left me wondering what the attraction was. I had nothing of value to offer. Even if I didn't know why, I did know His whole world was built around me. Even the cross had to do with me.

Not wanting to face my miniscule fear seemed silly now. I mean, every time I trusted Him, it turned out good, ultimately. Almighty stood beside me silently, letting me reason things out in my mind. "All right," I said at last. "Take me to the cliff, I want to jump." Joy flooded His face. My decision caused excitement in Him, and I watched His face radiate with a new energy.

So, Almighty carried me on His back for the long trip down the mountain. The way was icy and treacherous, the journey long. I couldn't have made it. No mere man could have. My tight grip around Him allowed His body heat to keep me relatively warm. I tucked my face into His neck and stayed protected from the elements.

After many days, icicles clung to His hair and sharp crystal shards had bloodied His hands. Yet when we reached the bottom, He seemed rejuvenated. I didn't get it. I tilted my head and asked, "Why are you so happy when you just completed a grueling climb down a huge, frozen mountain that tore up Your hands?"

He was already grinning, but His smile spread across His face. With sheer delight in His voice, He said, "I haven't been that close to you like that for a very long time. You depended on me to get you down the mountain and you clung to me the entire time, holding on for dear life. I loved it, it was magical."

His answer didn't surprise me, it was typical. He brought me back up to the edge of the precarious cliff. I looked at Him and then peered over the edge.

"Do you want me to go first," He asked.

"No," I moaned. "I just wanted to get it over with." The sooner I jumped the better. Hurling myself from the false safety of this desolate cliff into my pool of fears below was not a pleasant prospect, even though it was Almighty who was encouraging me to move toward a place of dread. I kept in mind He was the greatest source of comfort I knew. My heart sped up and I searched His eyes for affirmation. The righteous will live by faith, crept into my mind and did not leave. It overtook my thoughts. My feelings did not have to dominate me. I would do what I knew in my heart was going to be best for me.

Backing up to get a running start, I ran forward, straight into what terrified me the most. I jumped off the cliff, the wind whipping around me as I did a freefall for what seemed the longest moment of my life. The ocean water hit hard but felt like liquid silk oozing over every pore. It saturated me, detoxifying every obstinate emotion. I felt the water sliding up and down my skin, washing me. "I did it!" Wanting to laugh, I glanced up at Almighty. I was so happy. Was this really me? I had thought myself a coward.

Just then, the sun crept over the mountain peaks. It was a new day, a new era. I ached to see myself the way Almighty saw me—fearless and unflawed. Fear was gone. When I'd faced it boldly, it had vanished. Fear was actually afraid of me.

On the cliff high above, stood the small figure of Almighty. I just wanted to gaze at Him and keep gazing, drinking Him in, worshiping Him in my heart. Without warning, He threw Himself off the cliff, did two flips in the air and cannon balled into the ocean. His motions were brave and majestic. I felt nothing but love for Almighty. When fear was cast out, nothing but love remained.

He swam to me. "What are you thinking?"

"I want to do what You just did." I studied the top of the cliff and imagined myself doing multiple flips.

"I figured you would. Come on." He led me on a path around the backside of the mountain back up to the top in what seemed like only moments. There I was again, facing the waters below, this time with more boldness, but still with a twinge of anticipation. I let Him go first. This time He did three flips. This was going to be more intense than the last time. Taking a quick breath, I ran and flipped off the side into the water below. The rush was dynamic. I realized the greater the boldness that was required, the greater the pleasure of the experience.

As I hit the water and felt it glide over me, I sensed a powerful release. Release from all that had stopped me, all that had held me back. Freedom was mine. Almighty and I continued doing flips all day long until the sun went down. Even then, I didn't want to stop.

It occurred to me that Almighty knew what I didn't about the outcome of things. I saw one side and He saw the other. From then on, I wanted to rely on this mindset and on His perspective rather than my own. His was far better. In doing so, my life changed, and I experienced the exhilaration of moving from freedom to freedom.

CHAPTER 12

LIGHTNING DANCE

Around this time, chaos hit the world. There were wars and rumors of wars, destruction and confusion. I hid away as safely as possible, fearful like the rest of humanity, until one late afternoon a blackout hit. There was total loss of power and electricity, increasing the uncertainty.

We didn't know a bomb was lodged in one of the major official buildings in the city. A few hours after the blackout, it exploded, ripping apart everything around it. No one knew until it was too late. Many died and others were wounded. The destruction was severe, the confusion rampant, the chaos maddening. Throughout the night, I saw people running, screaming. Sounds of wailing filled the air at the loss of loved ones. With the blackout still intact, I cringed at the outcry of violence and rape.

Where was Almighty when all this was happening? I searched desperately for Him, venturing into the darkness and risking my own safety. I needed to find Him. I needed to reason with Him, needed to know everything would be all right.

Searching in the city near mountains of debris and rubble, I checked behind corners of buildings and even in dangerous dark alleys. Not finding Him in the city, I set out toward the forest. I cried for Him but there was no response. Stumbling on, I searched the oak grove and the banks of the river. I searched in all the meadows and anywhere I had ever known Him to be but couldn't find Him. Exhausted and in despair, I returned to the city.

What was Almighty up to? I felt restless, avoiding sleep. Stilling my thoughts, I remembered Almighty had built courage in me. From our time together, He had infused fearlessness. His confidence had rubbed off on me. Leaving my place of safety, I headed for the park to wrestle with my thoughts for the next few hours. Roaming through the park in the middle of a city, in the middle of a night scorched with hostility and cries of rape and chaos was not the wisest decision I could have made. Wisdom was not my forte this particular night.

Finding the fountain where people had thrown coins for wishes, I circled it, searching for meaning in the midst of despair. I followed the walkways and studied the dark silhouettes of trees, their leaves hanging down like a shroud. And then I saw Almighty. He lay asleep on a bench in the center of the park. Inching closer, I studied the form to make certain what I was seeing was accurate. It was Him. I couldn't believe my eyes. How could He be sleeping at a time like this?

The answer came swiftly. Even when Almighty was awake, He seemed in a constant state of rest. He was unfazed by, well, everything. In fact, fear and anxiety were not even in His vocabulary. His very essence combated those things and cast them out. I ran to Him and shook Him. "Almighty, get up, wake up," I cried frantically. He slowly opened His eyes and yawned. "Don't You care that people are dying?" I cried.

Recognizing me, He smiled and tried to pull me onto the bench to rest with Him. I was appalled, frustrated and shouted, "Why don't you react to this terror like everybody else."

"I'm not like anybody else," He responded in a slow steady tone.

Indignant, I retorted, "Well, I think You should be!"

He tilted His head back and started to chuckle, infuriating me. "If I was like everybody else, this world would be a terrifying place."

"It's a terrifying place right now," I shouted.

He stood, towering over me, eyes piercing my defiance. I melted, realizing in that moment, I had been rebuking Almighty. With gentle, but firm words, He said, "Eppy, why do you have so little faith?"

His words stopped my mouth. I couldn't speak, and I didn't understand what faith had to do with what was going on in the world. Horror surrounded us—chaos and darkness and misery. People were dying and suffering. Faith was having hope in the unseen, the confident expectation of coming good. How did that apply here?

I peered up at Almighty's face. He was filled with such bizarre serenity that it boggled my mind. I always felt like He knew things I didn't know about, like He saw beyond what I could, into another realm. Like He had a secret room in another world filled to the brim with untapped truths—truths that must be searched for like hidden treasure. I decided not to comment on the faith remark.

He lifted His eyes toward the smoke rising from the skyscraper in the center of the city. "Come on," He said, grabbing my hand and leading me away. He was taking me away from the city toward the wilderness. "I've longed for many years to bring you out to this wilderness and show you things about the intensity of my loving kindness toward you. There are things you have yet to learn about my feelings toward you that will bring you alive in a way that is still foreign to you."

I couldn't believe what I was hearing. We were in escape mode, running for cover and He was talking about taking me on a vacation and speaking in some kind of love language to me. "Almighty can't we just focus on what we're doing right now?" After I asked this, He remained silent for the next few hours of the journey.

We arrived in the wilderness. The air was so parched that I began breathing in dust. There were little desert plants scattered throughout the plain. Loose pebbles rolled across the dry ground when the intensity of the wind periodically blew. The wind sounded like a dying cow. It was hollow and empty. My throat was dry, and my body dehydrated. "I'm thirsty, Almighty," I said after hours of silence.

Almighty took me over to an odd-looking plant, small and green. He knelt down, broke it open and squeezed a clear, thick gel-like substance onto His fingers. He placed fingers inside my mouth and rubbed it on my tongue and then He squeezed out a little more and rubbed it on the outside and inside of my lips. This completely quenched my thirst. He didn't put any in His own mouth. Apparently, He wasn't thirsty.

We finally passed through the desert and came to a little river near the mountain cliffs. "We will camp out here," He said. He led me to a plum tree by the banks of the river. "You can sit here and wait for me and enjoy the plums." He pulled three of them off the tree and gave them to me. Then He took off into the woods. He left me there for hours. I was stranded with my thoughts under the fruit tree. I thought about Almighty and His ways. His ways were so far removed from my understanding, but I was continually intrigued by Him. I kept eating plums, wondering what was going to happen next. I almost fell asleep.

Almighty returned a few hours later with a pile of wood He had gathered and four dead fish He must have caught. He placed the wood on the ground and started a fire the primitive way, by rubbing sticks together. Then He put the fish on a stick and roasted them on the fire like marsh mellows. It was now evening. We ate and as soon as we finished, it began to rain, pouring down so hard it nearly extinguished the fire. I felt grateful to be somewhat sheltered by the trees that surrounded us.

Almighty instantly got up, ran out into the rain and raised His arms into the air. His face was turned up to the sky as if He were asking it to pour down harder. He began to rub His hands over His face and body, welcoming the feeling of the cold water pouring over Him. I watched Him. I couldn't take my eyes off of Him. Then I heard thunder and lightning. Sure enough, streaks of lightning began running across the sky. They bolted down, nearly hitting the spot where Almighty was enjoying the intimacy of the rain. They came faster and harder and Almighty began to dodge the firestorm. He looked at me. I didn't like that look, it made me nervous.

"Come. Dance with me Eppy," He said holding out His hand.

"What? Are you crazy? You may enjoy dodging lightning bolts, but I don't."

"Come on, Eppy," He said in a serious voice.

I was scared. This did not seem fun to me.

"Eppy, I want you out here with me." His voice was commanding. I had to go. I stood up and ran straight toward Him. When I reached Him, I flung my arms around His waist and clung onto Him. As soon as my body connected with His, He was happy. He put my hands on His shoulders and we danced in the rain. He seemed to be able to dodge lightning without trying. The lightning danced around us, and we danced around it. It was an adrenalin-induced dance. I finally looked away from Almighty and noticed all the lightning around us. It seemed like there was more lightning than rain. It lit the area around us like fireworks.

"Almighty I'm afraid," I cried. Almighty picked me up, wrapped my legs around His waist and continued to dance with me clinging to Him. I wrapped my arms around His neck and held onto Him tighter than before. He danced all night long and I fell asleep in His arms.

I woke up with the sun beating down, brightening the land and bringing warmth to the whole area. I was curled up under a shelter Almighty had made out of a tarp He had found. I didn't see Almighty, so I went down to the plum tree near the river and ate some plums. Almighty was swimming in the river. When He saw me, He got out and dried off.

"We have to go," He said taking my hand and beginning to lead me away.

"Where are we going now?" I whined digging my heels into the ground.

"I've set up a little cabin for you in the woods away from the city. You'll be safe there."

A cabin sounded good to me. So, I let Him take me there willingly, with no hesitation. It was another day's journey away. When we arrived, the sun was going down, but it was still bright enough to see the cabin. To me it looked less like a cabin and more like a hole in the ground. The door was on the side of a dirt hill. The cabin was literally made out of earth. Inside there was a bed, a fireplace, and a bathtub, but no furniture or pictures, and no kitchen or other rooms.

"Stay here and wait for me. I will return again," He promised. I knew I was going to get restless, but I obeyed. As He walked out the door, He glanced back at me, gave me wink and a smile and then He left.

CHAPTER 13

SICKNESS AND SURRENDER

I stayed in the house day after day, week after week and began to feel very lonely and isolated, like a hermit in the woods. I knew Almighty would return, but where was He now? I didn't like waiting. I thought about how all my family had abandoned me with the help of Adversary. My closest friends had died. Why was I stuck in this hole in the ground all alone? I grew very angry. What had begun with a tiny seed, a thought, a heartbreak, was now taking root.

For the next two weeks, I heard noises outside the cabin as though someone was prowling around. It felt like someone was spying on me, watching me, studying me. I didn't leave the cabin, even during the day. One evening, I looked out my window and saw him. Adversary ran around the yard like a wild animal. Even though he had attacked me and nearly taken my life, a boldness came over me. In a rush of rage, I raced outside and began throwing rocks. "Get out!" I screamed. "You ruined my life, took my family, destroyed my dreams."

He hid behind a tree dodging the rocks. "I've done nothing. You should be angry with your family. They left of their own free will. Even more than that, you should be angry with Almighty. He could've prevented any and all of these things from happening. You think He's so involved with you, but He's not. He doesn't care Eppy! I don't understand for the life of me why you're so enamored with Him. He leads you around by the throat. He's got you in a chokehold, and you like it. You follow Him around like a little puppy who's finally found an owner. You make me sick. Don't you see what's going on?"

The rock fell from my hand. His words made me feel weak. It was true. Almighty was dominating, but He was also freakishly tender, which was a very potent combination. But was it really wrong for a perfect, all-powerful, all-knowing Being to be dominating? Especially when He is utterly and totally selfless and completely interested in the redemption of mankind, even at the expense of His own skin? To me, it seemed fitting.

Did I really follow Him around like a puppy? The more I thought about it, the angrier I got. I was angry with my family and angry with Almighty for doing nothing to prevent the heartbreak of abandonment and death. I was also angry with myself for being such a follower.

One of the worst consequences of this thinking was that bitterness began to grow on the inside, making me physically sick. It started with a fever and cold sweats. My body ached all over like the flu. My head ached and throbbed relentlessly. All I could do was lie in bed. I felt the disease deep inside my heart. It was like cancer. I started to break out in sores all over my body—oozing puss-filled abscesses. It was horribly painful. I was stricken and afflicted. The worse I got, the angrier I became, which in turn made me even sicker. It was a horrid cycle. I grew pale. I was at death's door.

I didn't call out to Almighty, partly because I was angry with Him, but also because I felt so disgusting. I didn't want Him to see me in this condition. I was ashamed of myself. I knew it was my fault. Finally, I curled up in a ball and waited to die. I felt helpless, and I was. As I lay there one night, I heard galloping in the distance. Was it Almighty? I hadn't called for Him.

Maybe this noise was a hallucination, or the grim reaper coming to take me away. It wouldn't have surprised me. Why did I not call for Almighty? He was so good to me. It was stubbornness and pride. I was holding onto it like a metal shield, but now it was closing in on me like an iron maiden ready to bleed me dry. This unforgiveness was killing me from the inside out. The bitterness was drying up my bones and turning them to powder.

As the sound of the horse grew louder, I knew it was Almighty. I hid under my covers. He didn't knock on the door, just let Himself in.

"Eppy," Almighty whispered. When He said my name, it sent chills through my body. My spirit longed for Him. "Why are you hiding from me?" He asked softly.

"I don't want you to look at me. I'm disgusting. Just go away and let me die."

He ignored my request, came over to the bed and pulled off the blanket I was hiding under. I didn't even know how horrible I looked. I hadn't looked in the mirror for a while. I was so pale, and the sores had spread across my entire body, even covering my face. Almighty didn't seem the least bit repulsed when He saw me. In fact, His face showed He had the same amount of love and passion He'd always had. I had expected Him to feel squeamish, but He reached down to touch me. I slapped His hand away.

"Eppy," He said kneeling beside the bed, "you need an operation. You've let bitterness and unforgiveness breed inside you like cancer, and it's killing you."

"But there's nothing I can do about it," I argued. "I'm angry."

"I know that's why I'm here. You can't heal yourself, that's true, but there is one thing you can do."

"What's that?"

"Give me permission to remove it from you."

I thought about that. It was really weird, but even though it was killing me, there was a part of me that didn't want to let it go. I wanted revenge. Letting it go would make me feel powerless, and yet I was powerless now in a sick cancer-like state. I knew that whatever Almighty did, or told me to do, always turned out for the good ultimately. So why would this be any different? I looked up into His eyes. He loved me. He had proven it time and time and time again. "Alright," I said finally, battling my reluctance. "Take it out."

He smiled and pulled out a knife. My smile disappeared. "Wait a minute," I shouted. "I didn't know you were going to have to cut into me."

"Of course. How do you think I'm going to get the disease out?" Almighty gathered wood from outside the cabin and made a fire. He took the knife and heated the blade in the fire to sterilize it.

I stared at the blade. "Is this going to hurt?"

"Well, do you have some kind of anesthesia stashed somewhere around this place?"

"No," I said.

"Then, yeah it's going to hurt."

I began to sweat. What in the world had I gotten myself into? I didn't know He was going to do real surgery on me.

"Are you ready?" He asked, walking over to the bed.

"No, I'm not!"

"I'm a skillful surgeon," He said in a soothing voice. "Trust me, Eppy."

In that moment, I did trust Him. Everything His hands did had passion and purpose, which sometimes included pain. But I was still resistant. I couldn't help it. A knife was coming toward me. I kept pushing His hand away and trying to avoid the knife. He reached down to grab my hand and comfort me. "It's ok, Eppy," He said in a soothing voice. "I want to heal you. Will you let me? You don't know the joys that are on the other side of forgiveness and the horror that's attached to bitterness."

I realized in that moment this was something I had to willingly surrender to. He would not force it on me. This was completely and totally my choice. I had to put my emotions aside and let Him do this work in me by faith. "Alright, go ahead. Heal me."

He tore open the shirt that covered my bitterness and with His knife, headed straight for my heart. Even though I was awake, I couldn't see what He was doing inside me. As the knife cut in, pain ran through my body. I thought I might pass out. Thankfully, it became easier after the initial incision. In fact, once He started working on my heart, I barely felt the pain.

As He began removing bits of bitterness, I felt the symptoms of my affliction diminishing. The ache was gone. The sickness was being removed. I studied Almighty's eyes. He was focused, concentrating on His task. I realized even though this was painful, it was still Him that was doing everything. All I had to do was surrender. I patiently lay still as He carefully and skillfully removed every bit of unforgiveness that I had allowed to fester in the deepest parts of me. When He finally finished, He carefully closed up the wound and sewed the surface of my skin shut.

A complete renewal came over me. It was as though I had been asleep for centuries and had finally awakened, having experienced the rest of kings. I felt like I had sweated out and detoxed every awful thing. I was cleansed like a newborn baby. It was a messy operation though. I was covered in blood that had splattered everywhere. "What now Almighty?"

"You did good Eppy," He said, putting His hand affectionately on my head. "You rest for a bit. I'm going down to the river. I'll be back."

I lay on my bed, still covered in blood, thinking about His words: "You did good Eppy." I really didn't do anything. From start to finish, He did everything, even the way He prepared me and comforted me by speaking gently to me. He had healed me. Maybe He was proud of me for surrendering. In all reality, I was the one who had made myself sick and allowed myself to stay in that condition through stubbornness and pride. Almighty always put a positive spin on everything.

He came back from the river with a huge animal skin made into a bag and filled with water. He emptied it into a pot and heated it over the fire, then poured it in the tub. He made several trips back and forth between the river and the cabin hauling water and heating it up. Finally, the tub was filled to the brim and steaming. Almighty carefully removed all my bloody clothes, needing to cut some of them off with His knife. He carried me over to the tub and set me into it.

The water felt like a warm liquid blanket covering me. It seemed to soak into my pores like healing balm. I closed my eyes and smiled. I was so thankful He didn't leave me in my miserable condition. Almighty took off His shirt, soaked it in the water, and began to wash my wounded body. When He was finished, all the sores that had previously covered my skin had vanished. My skin became like a child's.

When He finished cleansing me, He set me on the rug by the fire to dry off. I watched the flames dancing to the rhythm of the new song that was in my heart. The sparks glided through the air like angels. Almighty stared at the fire with a big goofy grin on His face, as if He heard the music in my head.

"I have something for you," He said.

"Really?" I responded excitedly.

"I'll be right back," He said, going outside to His horse where He had packages hidden in the saddlebags on each side. He came back holding a long white dress. It had crocheted lace with gold woven into the borders.

"Where did you get this?" I gasped. I had never seen a garment so beautiful.

"I made it," He said simply. He slipped it over my head, and immediately I felt like royalty. He pulled out silk shoes spun from golden thread. They slipped over my feet and fit snuggly like a glove. Next, He pulled out a gold chain and placed it around my neck. I wanted to dance in front of the fire. The final item He had hidden away was white with lines of blue and gold on the ends near the tassels. He wrapped it around me like a shawl and we sat down by the fire again.

"Almighty," I whispered.

"Yes, Eppy," he said, His voice endearing.

"Where did you put the knife you used to cut me open and take out my disease?"

"I washed it in the river and put it in my saddle bag."

"Oh," I said quickly.

"It's a special knife to me," He continued.

"Why?"

"Well, it's the same knife I used to carve your name into my hand."

"Oh." I was surprised He verbalized that so casually, as if it was no big deal.

CHAPTER 14

WHO ARE YOU?

"Eppy, do you know what tomorrow is?"

"No, I don't." In the past couple months, I had lost track of all days and any significant factors attached to them.

"Tomorrow is the first day of the New Year."

"Really?" I answered, wondering why it mattered.

"Yes," He said staring into the fire, studying the flames.

"Is there a reason why you're telling me this?" I asked, knowing there probably was.

"I was just thinking about how people make resolutions at the beginning of every year. Everybody has such a built-in desire to change, to become better or different."

"Is that good?"

"The intentions are good, but it usually doesn't last very long. Besides, the kinds of resolutions people make usually aren't of any eternal significance."

"What kind of resolutions would You make?"

"I don't change," He answered. "It would be very bad for everyone if I did."

I moved closer to the fire. "What kind of resolutions would you make for me?"

He looked at me and started laughing. I realized He had been waiting for me to ask—that's what this whole thing was about. He moved closer and put His arms around me, stroking my back gently.

I wondered what He was going to say. Maybe He secretly had a whole bunch of things I needed to work on and change. I was sure it was going to take the next few hours for Him to unload everything He wanted to see change in me this year. I started to feel anxious.

"Well, since you're asking," He said, drawing out his answer. "There is one thing."

I breathed a sigh of relief that there was only one thing. That was good, but how could He narrow all of my many issues down to one? I became really curious about what this one thing was. He became silent, and I couldn't contain my curiosity. "What's on your heart?" I prodded.

"If I could ask one thing of you this year, it would be this," He continued. "Cling to me like never before. Wrap your legs around my waist and your arms around my neck and hold onto me like a little child, and don't let go."

I met His eyes in surprise. It didn't sound like any normal resolution I had ever heard of, but then, Almighty wasn't any ordinary Joe Shmo. His thought processes ran somewhere far beyond the blue. I started to smile. It was so like Him to ask that of me. It might have sounded like an easy request, except I so easily strayed away, like the little lost sheep. Even when I wasn't wandering off, I didn't quite comprehend the depth of intimacy He wanted to have with me.

"You know, Eppy, everything else comes from that one thing—all power and victory, faith and passion, boldness and beauty. When you are holding onto me, my life force flows through you."

I thought about Almighty's request as He left the cabin to gather more wood for the fire. Would this next year be better if I clung to Him harder? Would it be different? I heard Almighty chopping wood in the front yard, the harsh sound of the ax slicing through the logs, splitting them into smaller pieces. The rhythm of the ax was melodic. It sounded like a drumbeat, a battle cry.

My mind wandered to the pounding sound of the spikes driven into His hands so long ago, mangling them. I thought about my losses this last year. Friends were killed, my family deserted me, I lost my livelihood, and I was driven into the woods like a hermit, like an outcast to live in solitude and isolation.

Then I heard the pounding of the ax and remembered all the adventures I'd had with Almighty this year. It's been a good year, I thought. And the more I cling onto Almighty, the better it's going to be. I couldn't help smiling when I thought about Him. He brought a joy to me that was beyond my understanding.

Almighty came back into the cabin and piled the wood so high it covered an entire wall. "That ought to last you for a while," He said. He came over to me, kissed me on the forehead and stared into my eyes for a moment and then He left.

I became excited about the New Year. What would He teach me? Where would He take me? What would we talk about? I made a decision in my heart that I would cling to Almighty tighter than I ever had before.

So, I pursued after Him and He pursued after me. My heart became like soft clay being molded in His hand. Our interaction was a continuous, daily, regular thing. Each morning, I awoke with anticipation in my heart. I couldn't wait to hear His voice, feel His love. Sometimes I arose in the middle of the night just to tell Him how much I adored Him. We met regularly out in the wilderness. There He would build a fire and I would sing songs to Him, and he would sing back to me. After spending a day with Almighty, my whole face glowed.

One time in the wilderness, I knew we were searching for each other simultaneously, a search that lasted all day. I felt the sun beating down as I raced behind mountain cliffs and down forest pathways. Wherever I went, I felt Him just behind me or just ahead of me. I loved the excitement of searching for Him. It drew out the anticipation of the experience.

I finally found Him behind some church ruins in the middle of a field. The building was exceedingly old. Cement blocks and pieces of wall were surrounded by grass. Abundant wildflowers made the whole scene look like a piece of art. We ran and embraced each other, not wanting to let go.

As the sun was setting, we sat down in the middle of the ruins and Almighty made a fire. I didn't speak much, just wanting to enjoy His presence. We sat by the fire across from each other and smiled, speaking to each other with our eyes, literally having a conversation with our expressions and body language.

Almighty moved closer to me, keeping His eyes on the fire. Suddenly He pinned me down and began to wrestle with me. His intensity was startling. We wrestled all night long. We stopped as the sun was rising, peaking from behind the clouds with a little sparkle of light. I lay by the fire that had gone out hours ago. I stared up at Almighty, not knowing what to think about the way we had just spent the night.

He looked at me endearingly.

"Who are you?" I asked suddenly.

He began gently stroking my head. "I am the one who dwells in eternity, and I also dwell with those who have a broken spirit and a humble heart."

"But who are you?" I insisted, not feeling satisfied with His answer.

He looked away, closed His eyes and sighed as if meditating on something. Then He looked down at me again. "You know who I am Eppy. I AM."

He had used those words to describe Himself before. There was fire in those words.

"Almighty, I just want to be your servant forever."

He smiled. "Back in the day, they had a name for a willing servant by choice. It's called a bondservant. A servant was usually released after working for somebody for a period of time. But if that servant loved his master and was content to stay with him, his master would take him to the doorpost and drive an earring through his ear. This symbolized that he was a willing servant to his master's for the rest of his life."

"I want to be your servant. Pierce my ear," I said jumping up excitedly.

"Really?" He asked.

"Yes, with all my heart."

"Alright, I'll have to find something to pierce you with. I'll be back."

I was exuberant to be identified with Almighty in this way. He seemed nonchalant about it though. He just didn't seem super stoked for some reason.

He came back with a little piece of wood He had whittled into a small spike. "This will work for now," He said. "In a day or two, I will bring you a gold earring. He laid me on the ground and placed my ear against a flat rock. He drove the wooden spike into the top part of my ear. It went in smoothly and didn't hurt nearly as much as I thought it would.

"Yes, I'm officially your bond servant," I said jumping up in enthusiasm.

"I wanted you to be my wife," He muttered under His breath, walking over to pick up sticks to start the fire.

Did I hear him correctly? That's an absurd notion. I couldn't begin to understand the concept of that kind of relationship with Almighty. I couldn't have that kind of oneness with Him, so why would He even want it with me? It was impossible.

Almighty looked troubled as He built the fire. He didn't look at me but was totally engaged in gathering wood and setting it up. It was obvious He was reading my thoughts. Why wasn't He satisfied with me being his bondservant? I thought that would bring Him pleasure. Maybe it did, but it seemed He kept pushing the envelope, wanting more and more of me. I knew Almighty had a deeply artistic, creative mind and He thought toward the impossible. He was a genius. But this just didn't feel right. How could He possibly want this?

Almighty reignited the fire and we both sat staring at it in silence.

"You don't even call me daddy," He said, continuing to fix His gaze toward the fire.

I had forgotten about our communion night and how He told me that I am His adopted child, how He wanted to be related to me. Even that seemed so beyond belief. Sometimes when something was hard to grasp, I would end up disregarding it and allowing it to become a surface reality, not giving it the opportunity to penetrate deeply into my soul.

"I'm going to a quiet place to pray," He said gently.

"Almighty, who are you praying to?" I asked.

He gave me a big smile. "I am going to commune with myself," He said with a laugh. He started to walk away, and then He stopped and turned back around, His voice passionate, "Eppy. I love you so much, more than you'll ever know." Then He turned back and walked away.

I stayed at that spot for days. The fire went out and I didn't bother to start it again. Instead, I curled up in the cold dirt and wrestled with my thoughts. Almighty's words prevailed. You don't even call me daddy, echoed in my mind. Those words rose above all other words or concepts trying to make their way into my mind. Almighty wanted all of me, everything. I looked up at the moon. It was so bright and full and glorious. I imagined Him hanging it in the sky. It glowed around the whole area where I was lying. My soul began to fill up with such longing that I couldn't contain it. I wanted to be His child. It was my greatest desire. I stood up and began to pace back and forth under the moon like a mad man. My thoughts suddenly became very verbal and very loud.

Almighty also talks to Himself, I thought after I had finished having a five-part conversation with myself. There was nothing I could do to understand Almighty. I just had to believe. There was nothing I could do to be good enough for Him. I just had to receive. That's what this whole thing was about.

Almighty was not like anyone else, that one thing I had come to realize with absolute certainty. He was powerful and pure, potent and perfect. I couldn't have a relationship with Him and expect it not to affect me. I couldn't be with Him and leave His presence unchanged. He had chosen me. His pull on my soul was indefinable. His pursuit of my heart was undeniable. And His passion to show me kindness was indescribable.

The night had just begun. It would be hours and hours before the sun came up, but I couldn't wait. I needed to find Almighty and tell Him I wanted to be His child. I would forever think of Him as my father. I began my journey in the dark with the moon as my light. I forged through the woods and followed a path that kept getting higher and higher in elevation. I didn't know where I was going, but I knew in my heart Almighty was on the other end. I felt lost but finally realized I was following a trail leading to the top of a mountain.

The stars became visible. My anxious heart began to beat faster, knowing very soon I would be in Almighty's presence. I tried to prepare myself for what was coming. I knew something was. What would it be like to take down all my walls and to allow His love to possess me? It was almost too much for me to handle. I finally arrived at the top of the mountain where I came to a large plateau with trees sparsely scattered around as in a park.

Then I saw Him sitting on the edge of the mountain staring at the night sky, praying. I wondered if His prayers had affected my thought processes over the last few days. His voice seemed like it was always in my head. When I saw Him, a wellspring of emotion began to stir up in the deepest part of me. I needed Him desperately. I was lost without Him. Tears began to fill up my eyes. I started running toward Him. "Almighty, I want you to be my daddy!" I cried.

He turned and saw me running toward Him. His face glowed with excitement. When I reached Him, He picked me up and held me in His arms like a child.

"I want you to be my daddy," I said again.

He pulled a ring out of His pocket while holding me around His waist.

"I want you to be my wife," He said.

I became lightheaded.

The ring He was presenting to me was made of silver. It was thick and heavy. It had striped lines intersecting each other all around the band. On the top of the ring were tiny diamonds that sparkled like the stars. They grouped together to form a heart.

"The stripes on this ring will remind you of the scourging that I took when I went to the cross, and because of my suffering you will shine forever like the little diamonds on this ring."

I couldn't speak, but my heart was saying yes. So Almighty slipped the ring on my finger without me having to utter a word.

In that moment, I understood something for the first time in my life. The work of redemption that Almighty did on the cross is a marriage proposal to the souls of mankind. Anyone who desired Him could come. He calls everyone individually. He knocks at the door of their heart day after day, night after night, waiting, longing, praying and pleading, "Come and reason with me, though your sins are scarlet, they will be white as snow, though they are red like crimson they will be as wool."

He put me down and we sat next to each other under the stars. I stared at the ring in amazement. I think I finally understood who Almighty is. He is the One who makes the impossible possible.

"Almighty, what happens now? How do we get married?"

"I am going ahead to set up a place for us to dwell together forever. Right now, you are flesh and blood, and I am light and perfection. We can't dwell together in the kind of oneness that I desire without transformation. You will be changed into spirit and be made perfect.

"I have become like you in order to make it possible for you to become like me. I was rich in eternity, dwelling in blissful perfection, but I become poor, taking on human flesh and dying a criminal's death, so that you, through my poverty might become rich and come with me into eternity.

"When you become like me, you will be relieved of sin and misery, suffering and sickness, empty pleasure, limited intelligence, hopelessness and disappointment. Every terrible heartbreaking thing will be wiped away because it will not stand in my presence. In my presence is fullness of joy and at my right hand are pleasures forever more."

"Where exactly is this place that you are taking me?"

"It's in another dimension."

That didn't surprise me at all. "What is it like there?" I asked.

"It's an incomprehensibly beautiful city. In it is the fulfillment of the deepest, most hidden desires in the hearts of mankind, without the disappointment of having arrived with nothing left to hope for. This place is more real than the world you've come to know. The depths that are experienced there will make this life seem one-dimensional. Nothing will be mundane or routine. Every day will be a new experience, a new adventure.

"You will constantly be developing new connections and relationships with those living in the city. You will feed off everyone's energy, creating new levels of joy and peace and ecstasy. This is only possible because everyone will be connected to the life source of all energy—me. There will be no need for a sun because I will be the light source, the warmth and the nutrition for your spirits.

"Since everyone is unique, each person will have a special task and purpose. Every soul will be filled with passion. Each person will have a new body and their personality will be truly seen on the outside. Your soul will literally take on a face. Everyone will be delighting in me and therefore have an innate ability to delight in each other.

"People will be so happy they will thank their enemies for the suffering they caused because it worked out for them a far more exceeding and eternal weight of glory. There will be dancing and worship, music and joy, but it will all be done in a constant state of rest, eternal rest. And when you arrive there, you will feel at home for the first time in your entire existence because you will be with me forever."

When Almighty finished speaking, I prostrated myself before Him. I could do nothing else. I realized in that moment that the worship of any other being would be utter foolishness.

Almighty leaned down and whispered in my ear. "I'll always be with you, My Bride, you're never alone. All day long, my arms are stretched out to you because I love you with an everlasting love."

When I looked up, He was gone. He left me there gazing at the stars. The one that He had named My Bride, after me, outshined all the others in the sky. I lay still and silent, glowing with a smile reaching from ear to ear, anticipation coursing through my spirit. Nothing else mattered anymore except this one thing: Almighty was coming to take me away. Until then, I would spend my life delighting in Him and waiting for that day.

ABOUT THE AUTHOR

Rebekah Schwep, singer, songwriter, and poet is delighted to share with you her first story, Adventures with Almighty. Consumed with the goodness of God's grace, this theme is constant throughout all her creative endeavors.

She is always thrilled to receive notes from readers who have benefitted from her work at: www.rebekahschwep.weebly.com.